The Mohicans
Last of their Tribe
Johannah Jahn

For my father, who first introduced me to the original masterpiece.

"For by grace you have been saved through faith; and this is not your own doing, it is the gift of God"

Ephesians 2:8 (RSVCE)

Contents

Preface

James Fenimore Cooper wrote *The Last of the Mohicans* in 1826. The story was ahead of its time, but was far from flawless. Part of my adaptation includes removing the racial stereotypes written into the original. However, this does not mean racism is absent from the story. We need to remember that it takes place in 1757, a time period in history when prejudice was rife. If these themes, along with violence and brief mentions of sexual assault, make you uncomfortable, this story is probably not for you.

10 June 1757

I

The Conversation

14:32

C ora and Alice Munro sat in the study of their manor, each
amusing themselves in their own particular way. It was a large
study, with a desk by the windows and two crimson sofas sitting opposite each other, adjacent to the desk. The ladies matched the elegance
of the room. Cora, the elder, wore a light green dress, and Alice wore
a pink one.

The sun shone through the tall window behind them, illuminat-
ing the words atop Cora's copy of *Robinson Crusoe*. After finishing
a chapter, Cora laid the novel down, pressing her cloth bookmark
between the pages.

"I'm going to write to Papa." She looked up at her sister, who was
working on an embroidery piece. Alice's blue eyes met her sister's
honey-brown eyes.

"To say what?"

"That we are going to meet him, of course." Cora moved to the
table to pen such a letter. Alice's eyes shifted to her embroidery again.

"Is our journey set in stone, Cora?"

"Alice, I know you would rather he came home, and I understand
your feelings. I wish the army would dismiss him and relieve him of

his duty, but that won't happen for some time. The longer we wait, the more likely we are to lose him before we see him again."

"You're right, of course. We need to see him again, but why must it be there? It's such a dangerous, savage land."

Cora raised an eyebrow at this comment. "How can you speak like this about a place we have never been?"

"They are all heathens, Cora. Bloodthirsty savages, it says so in the papers."

"Alice!" Cora stood to correct her sister's speech. "How can you say such a thing? To assume something so vicious without ever meeting one of them. To assume they are all the same and untrustworthy because of their complexion. Alice, come now. I've taught you better than that."

Alice looked at her lap, becoming very interested in her fingernails.

"Cora, everyone who has been there also speaks of the savagery; it must be true."

"And if everyone said that those with blonde hair were savages, would you think yourself one?"

Alice shook her head, biting her lip.

Then she stood, meeting her sister's eyes with a teasing smile. "And what happens, my dear sister, when I reach the Americas and instantly die at the hands of the French?" She feigned being shot and collapsed into the chair she had just occupied. Cora shook with laughter. She grasped her sister's hands and squeezed them.

"Absolutely not, flower. I refuse to allow you to die a maid!"

Suddenly, the door to the study swung open, and the girls' governess strode in. Her hands on her hips before she ever opened her mouth.

"Cora Munro! What on earth are you discussing with your sister?" Both girls dropped their eyes to their laps, blushing.

"We were just joking, ma'am. It was nothing in earnest," Cora said, looking up at their governess from beneath her eyelashes.

"Lord help me! All I ask from you is that you behave like proper young ladies until your father returns, and I may suffer you no longer!" She spun on her heel and left the room, closing the door behind her.

Cora turned to Alice, smirking. "Why must she always be such an old witch?"

Alice snorted before throwing her hand over her mouth to stifle the sound of her laughter.

"Cora, you mustn't say such things!" She looked over at her older sister, who was imitating the governess's scowl perfectly.

"And why not? She treats us as if we are children, and we are both of marriageable age." Alice's gaze returned to her lap.

"As if that matters," she muttered under her breath.

"What do you mean by that, my flower? You are never in want of a partner at dances and balls, and there are always gentlemen callers here to see you."

"They don't notice me, Cora; they only have eyes for you."

Cora shook her head. "Alice, I know for a fact that Hector Bennet is in love with you."

"He is not!" Alice protested. "He barely speaks when we're together."

"All the more proof that he loves you, flower. He is nervous in your presence. Besides, Lieutenant Harchfield told me last Friday that Private Bennet has been asking all the non-commissioned officers how to get the attention of a certain young lady," Cora said, waggling her eyebrows.

Alice blanched. "Surely not. I doubt he meant me."

"Believe what you want, my flower, but I'm more certain that he loves you than I am that your hair is blonde."

Alice chortled, thumbing her golden curls. "And what am I meant to do if it is true?" she asked.

"What are you meant to do? What is he meant to do? Engaging you is entirely his responsibility."

"Not with getting his attention, Cora. With *not* getting his attention. I certainly do not desire it."

"Whyever not, flower?"

"He's just…Well, he's just so young." Cora raised an eyebrow at her sister's comment.

"Young? Alice, he's one year your senior. If he's young, what kind of man are you looking for?"

"Cora, perhaps I am meant to be with a different kind of man, someone less green."

"Ah, I see." Cora smiled. "You want an officer! That is very well, Alice. As the daughter of a lieutenant colonel, you may have an officer."

Alice shook her head. "No, Cora, that's not what I meant. I only meant… the soldiers are all so primped and perfect, sending us arranged compliments and never going a day without shaving."

"This is true. I will admit I never pictured you being the type to hate such a model."

"It is a rather new opinion, I think," Alice said.

Cora laughed.

"That is something that comes with growing up, I suppose."

Alice sighed.

"Hopefully, it's not me he desires attention from, and this is all moot."

"You shall see tonight, my flower. Watch his eyes, it is easy to tell a man's intentions by watching his eyes."

"And what would romantic feelings look like in the eyes, Cora?"

"You will know when you see it, flower."

11 June 1757

2
The Mohicans
21:15

T he buckskin-clad scout sat beside his surrogate father, offering him his water skin. The old chief accepted it and took a small drink, nodding his thanks.

"Have you spoken with Uncas[1] about his life recently, my father?" Hawkeye asked in the Mohican tongue. The chief looked up at him, his aged eyes stern and solemn.

"Uncas knows his future, Hawkeye. What else is there for me to say?"

"His future is not so clear." Hawkeye placed a bit of spruce resin in his mouth. "Would you have him live a celibate life, never to bring children into the world?" He began working the resin with his teeth until it became pliant.

"And why should my son marry? No child of his can truly carry on our line. Our family and tribe will die with him, regardless of whether

---

1. The name Uncas means "Fox," and Cooper likely based the name on a Mohegan sachem from the early 1600s.

he has children," Chingachgook[2] said, carving away at a small chunk of wood from a downed tree.

"How can you say that, Sagamore? The Turtle people in the north may not be Mohicans, but they are Delaware, just like you." Hawkeye took a long drink from his canteen, sweat from the hot summer's night thick on his forehead and soaking his brown hair.

"My white son does not understand. Our tribe cannot be sustained by mingling with other tribes, no matter how similar. Uncas may choose a wife from another tribe, but none of those children have the right to call themselves Mohicans."

"Would it not be better to retain some Mohican blood, no matter how small, than lose it forever? Why have you yourself not considered going north and finding a new wife?"

Chingachgook raised a hand. "Enough, Hawkeye! I cannot produce another Mohican child, and I will never forget Apanii.[3]"

Hawkeye looked at his hands. Whenever Chingachgook brought up his fallen wife, the conversation stalled. Hawkeye knew how much her death had affected his father. The man could not hunt for a week, surviving only on the fish from the lake where they had camped. Hawkeye had only been eight years old at that time, with limited hunting abilities. In fact, the experience had forced him to go out and learn how to shoot.

"Father, I understand how you feel. I barely knew Apanii, but I know she would not want you wasting away, refusing a woman's touch just because you lost her. And she certainly would not want you

---

2. The name Chingachgook means "Big Snake" in Lenape.

3. In *The Deerslayer* we learn that Chingachgook's wife is called Wah-ta-wah. It was changed here for thematic purposes.

to let your race die out for her sake. A Mohican with Delaware blood is still a Mohican."

When Chingachgook remained silent, Hawkeye relented, not wanting to upset him further. Both of the men stilled at the sound of the leaves rustling. Uncas emerged from the woods, the white feathers in his hair standing out against the dark night.

"I am here, Father." Uncas took a seat between Chingachgook and Hawkeye. Hawkeye glanced at his father before turning to his brother.

"Do you plan on marrying or coupling, Uncas?" Hawkeye asked, ignoring Chingachgook's glare.

Uncas' eyebrows raised at such a question.

"Why does my brother want to know?"

"You will be the last of your kind, Uncas, unless you have children. The Turtle people in the north are the nearest you will find to Mohicans. If you procreate with them, your race may yet survive."

"If I ever meet a woman I truly love, I shall pair off. I suppose if we are ever near those villages, that may happen, but we have not been that far north in a decade. Besides, none of those children would truly be Mohicans."

Hawkeye huffed, realizing he couldn't convince his adoptive family of his point. He leaned his back against a nearby tree and picked some meat off the bird Uncas had shot that morning.

His father may have been right. No true Mohicans would ever be born, but a half-Mohican could save the race, carrying on the blood of so many sachems who had passed.

3
The Ball

22:27

"I fear I shall not see you for some time, Lieutenant Harchfield," Cora said. The man's gloved hand matched up with hers as they inched around the couple in the middle of the circle. "My sister and I are to travel to the Americas to visit our father. Our ship departs on Friday."

Harchfield's eyes lit up. "What happy news, Miss Munro! I shall also be traveling to the Americas rather soon, in fact. We will depart on Monday morning. I was dreading telling you. But now you are setting out as well, perhaps we shall see each other when we get there!"

"How fortunate!" Cora beamed. "We will be going up the Hudson to Fort Edward, where we will take the road to Fort William Henry. What about you? Where will you be?"

Harchfield grinned.

"I am stationed at Fort William Henry, as are Miller, Garfield, and Bennet. So we will probably be taking the same trip as you. Perhaps General Webb will even allow us to act as escorts for you."

"General Webb?" Cora asked.

"The commanding officer at Fort Edward. He can be quite brutal sometimes, very much the military type."

Cora chuckled. "I think, as the daughter of a lieutenant colonel, I'd be rather used to the 'military type'." She covered her grin with her fan.

Harchfield smiled. The song ended, and he bowed to her; she curtsied in return. He led her to the side of the room where Alice sat, waiting for her. After delivering her to her sister, Harchfield walked away to join some of his comrades. The men teased him incessantly about popping the question to Miss Munro.

Lieutenant Alexander Harchfield had no interest in marrying Miss Munro. She was a beautiful woman with angular features, milky white skin, and silky, jet-black hair that fell in curled tresses over her shoulder. Her light brown, almost honey-colored eyes gleamed with amusement as he watched her from across the room. But she was just Cora. His best friend.

Cora was in much the same boat. Each time Alice asked her about her relationship with the lieutenant, she gave the same answer. He was a polite, perfectly polished man. Cora knew her father would approve of him, but she had only ever thought of him as a good friend.

Private Bennet escorted Alice to Cora's side, gave a small bow to the ladies, and walked off to join a group of privates.

"How was the dance, my flower?" Cora asked her sister. Alice met her sister's eyes, her lips curled up in a smirk.

"You were right, Cora. Every time he looks at me, his eyes change. His pupils dilate, and his eyebrows shoot up."

Cora put her hand up to her mouth, covering her laughter.

"Very good, and now you will always be able to spot affection in a man. So, what have you decided about the young private?"

"Hector is kind, a perfect gentleman. But he is green. I don't believe he has ever seen the field. As someone of such a junior rank, I worry about him dying the second he goes into combat. Cora, I do not believe I will ever marry. None of the men here are anything like what I want, and I will marry only for love," the girl said in a huff.

"I do admit, my flower, I never anticipated that you would be averse to marrying a beautiful soldier, but I am rather glad this is not the life you seek. But you will marry, do not fear that. We will go to America. All the men there will better suit your wishes, as they all survive the wilderness."

Alice smiled. "You're just saying that to make me excited to go!"

Cora nodded.

"Of course!" As the sisters began laughing, they saw Private Bennet walking over to join them.

He bowed as he approached. "Miss Munro, Miss Alice."

The ladies both inclined their heads. "Private Bennet."

"Might I have another dance with Miss Alice?" he asked, fidgeting with his hands. Cora's eyes shot to her sister's. Alice was flushed, her eyes staring at her lap. Cora looked back at Private Bennet.

"I am very sorry to have to steal her from you, sir, but my sister isn't feeling very well, and we're going to rest here for a while." Alice looked up at her sister, trying to hide her smile.

"Ah, I am very sorry to hear so. I pray that you feel better soon, Miss Alice." Bennet dipped his head as he walked away.

Alice tapped her sister's shoulder with her fan.

"Cora, you didn't have to do that."

"You mustn't encourage his affection, flower. You already danced with him once; a second would suggest that you reciprocate his feelings."

"You're right, of course. Thank you."

The girls conversed for the rest of the ball. Alice questioned her sister about many of the men who passed. Cora only responded with polite compliments of them, showing no particular affection for any of them outside her friendship with Alexander.

2 August 1757

4
Fort Edward

12:18

The boat that had taken them up the Hudson had now docked. The sun beat down on Cora and Alice as they stepped onto the New World for the first time. They lifted their skirts to step over the threshold of the boat, walking down the boardwalk to the ground, just outside Fort Edward.

The fort appeared friendly and welcoming, although a strange sight to the ladies. There were some similarities to their towns in Scotland: the same dirt roads that sent dust everywhere as men on horseback trotted by, and the same quaint shops lining the street. It was the people who looked different. The hem of every woman's dress was either covered in mud or dust, the civilian men wore no topcoats, and their collars were not starched.

Of course, the ladies were not perfectly polished either. They had spent two months on the boat, and aside from daily sponge baths, they hadn't cleaned themselves the whole time. Their hair stuck to their necks with sweat from the August sun, and Cora's curls had frizzed up from the humidity.

The soldiers guarding the gate laughed and joked with each other, and the gate was open. The sisters spotted colonials and soldiers alike walking around inside the gates. They squealed as they picked up their skirts and practically sprinted to the gate.

The gate-guards bowed, giving the pretty Munro sisters flirtatious smiles. "Ladies."

Cora and Alice grinned from ear to ear as they curtsied. "Gentlemen." They passed through the gate and began looking around. It was a cute little town, with ivy growing up the sides of the shop walls. There were soldiers everywhere, of course, but besides that, it felt like someone had plucked it right out of Scotland and placed it here in the American countryside.

"Should we explore?" Alice asked. She eyed all the small shops lining the street: a bakery, a hat shop, a bookstore, and a general store. Alice was fonder of perusing than actually buying anything, and for such a small town, there seemed to be plenty of shops.

"We can come back in a bit, my flower, but we need to locate General Webb first. If we delay, we may not be able to leave today." Cora grabbed her sister's hand. "Now, let's find someone who can direct us to the general's office." She looked up and down the street.

"There's an officer over—" Alice started before Cora began leading her toward a native who leaned against a wall. He seemed to be observing the street of pedestrians with a keen eye. He was quite striking, with sharp features that could cut glass. The sides of his head were shaved and his shiny black hair made a line down the center of his head, kept standing on edge with some kind of resin; the Mohawk style that Alice had seen on many of the natives in the fort. His eyes were dark brown, and they were filled with the light of laughter. He was wearing a loincloth, much like the other natives in the fort, but where he differed was his vest, which covered his back, shoulders, and most of his chest. There were thick red lines and three small black lines painted on his upper arms. He also had three black lines tattooed on his temple, extending out from his eyes.

The native raised an eyebrow when the ladies approached, but his eyes softened as Cora spoke.

"Excuse me, sir, I was hoping that you would direct my sister and me to General Webb's office."

"Cora... maybe we should ask a soldier," Alice said, cowering behind her sister at the sight of the man.

"Nonsense, my flower. This man surely knows his way around." Cora pulled her sister forward to stand next to her. "Is that not right, sir?"

The man smiled at her. "Yes, ma'am." He gestured for them to follow him.

"What is your name, sir?" Cora asked him, walking beside him rather than behind him. A group of women coming toward them gawked and turned to each other, whispering.

"My name is Magua,[1] but the French call me *Le Renard Subtil*," he said.

Cora's eyebrow raised. "Ah, the Subtle Fox. How did you come by that name?"

Magua smirked at this question. "For sneaking in and out of the French establishments," he said.

The group approached a building with two soldiers on guard duty. There was a young blond officer standing on the steps. He was a major, albeit a young one. His hair was pulled back in the ponytail typical of the English soldiers. The man had the appeals of a man of good breeding, with angular features and perfect grooming.

---

1. The name Magua was made up by James Fenimore Cooper.

"The Misses Munro?" the man asked, taking a step toward the ladies. Cora smiled and turned to Magua to say goodbye before speaking with the soldier. Magua's face fell as the soldier spoke the ladies' surname.

"It was very nice to meet you, Magua," Cora said, curtsying. Alice followed her lead and curtsied to the man before turning back to the major.

"I am Miss Cora Munro," Cora said, curtsying to the major. "And this is my sister, Miss Alice Munro." She motioned toward her sister. The man seemed to do a double take upon seeing the younger Munro sister. He bowed and extended a hand to Alice.

"I know you ladies are fresh off the boat, and America seems a different world, but I promise it will all feel more natural with time," he started. "But I must add that curtsying to the Indians is unnecessary. They are not gentlemen."

Cora's face remained neutral. "Of course, sir, but my sister and I have always treated any man who is respectful and kind as a gentleman."

The major nodded, trying to backstep. "Of course. May I introduce myself?"

"Naturally, Major."

"I am Major Heyward, and your father has sent me here to escort you to Fort William Henry, his post."

"It is good to meet you, Major. Will you be the only one escorting us?" The door of the building in front of them opened and two men walked out, just in time for the major to answer Cora's question.

"Lieutenant Harchfield! Private Bennet! What good luck!" Cora said, waving at the men. Both of them bowed and greeted the ladies.

"Are you acquainted with these gentlemen?" Major Heyward asked.

"Yes, they were stationed in Scotland before coming here, and frequented the social gatherings we attended," Cora explained.

"Ah, I see. Well then, you are in luck. These gentlemen will be the other members of our escort."

"Why such a small group? Are there no soldiers traveling to Fort William Henry?" Cora asked.

"There certainly are, but we are not to join them, as we cannot travel on the wagon trail. Because of the soldiers who travel there, it could become the object of Montcalm's attacks."

"I thought General Montcalm had no intention of coming out of Canada."

"We may discuss this further with General Webb," the major said, leading them into the building. Cora pursed her lips but followed. The inside of the building consisted of a single room, and a staircase leading up to what Cora presumed must be General Webb's bedroom. There was a desk in the corner, with paper scattered about and an inkwell in the corner. The walls showcased a few military portraits and a painting of King George II. A large map that depicted the surrounding area was behind the desk. The Hudson was drawn with a heavy blue line, and Lake George led up to Lake Champlain in a long light blue splotch. General Webb himself sat at the desk, but upon seeing the ladies entering the room, he stood up to greet them.

"Ladies, it is so very nice to meet you!" He approached them. He had on a powdered white wig, something Cora rarely saw. The soldiers she encountered on a regular basis wore casual clothing. When he was a few paces away from them, he bowed.

"I am General Webb, and I am very pleased to meet you. Though, I must say, I am surprised to see you here so soon. I received your letter not three days ago. Why did you not wait after writing, my dear?"

"I am very sorry if our presence is unwelcome, sir. We only wanted to see our father again. It has been quite some time since we last saw him, and he grows rather old now."

"If your father's old, what does that make me?" Webb questioned is a jovial tone. The wrinkles cut deep on his face, but it was his eyes that showed the man's age—red and underscored with heavy, dark circles.

Cora chuckled. "Why, not a day over thirty-five, sir." Webb chortled.

"Sir, when are we to depart? I understand the fort is a five-hour march, and it is past noon. If we expect to reach our father before night falls, we should probably leave rather soon," Cora said, glancing over at her sister, who was conversing with Major Heyward.

Webb shook his head. "You will be spending the night here, my dear. The back trail is where you will be traveling, as the wagon road is for military personnel only. The back trail is far longer, and you will need at least seven hours of travel time."

Cora frowned, but then nodded, not arguing this point.

3 August 1757

5
The Meeting

08:00

Colonel Munro strode into the tent, his escort accompanying him. General Louis-Joseph de Montcalm stood in the middle of the tent with his hands clasped behind his back. The man had a satisfied smirk plastered across his face. Munro removed his hat and bowed. The general returned the gesture with a flourish, sweeping his large black hat as he did so.

"Why, Colonel Munro, I am delighted you accepted my offer of negotiations."

Colonel Munro's lips thinned as he took in the man who had just laid siege to his fort.

"Negotiations? You requested we parley. I have no intention of negotiating anything. I take it, you are requesting I surrender my fort?" Munro questioned, lifting his chin.

"Why, of course, sir! You cannot seriously hope to continue defending this doomed fortress? We have you blocked on all sides. No one can get in, and no one can get out. You are alone, sir!"

Munro sneered. "You, of course, are forgetting that Fort Edwards is a short half-day walk from here. General, how can you say we are alone?"

"If that is what you are relying on, I think you should reconsider. With all due respect, your General Webb is not exactly renowned for his helpful nature."

"Be that as it may, my orders are to keep this fort or fall with it. And that I will do. You may attack and besiege me; you may even tear down my walls. But know this: should your men topple them, a thousand shall die in the breach!" Munro growled.

General Montcalm bit his lip. "Very well, Colonel. Understood."

Munro bowed to the general. "General Montcalm." He turned on his heel and exited the tent, joining his escort to walk back into the fort on the lake.

Montcalm sucked his cheek, annoyed. Colonel Munro was stubborn, and he had made it clear the fort would not fall without a fight. Montcalm would need every man he could get when he marched south to take Fort Edward; he could not afford to lose five hundred men on Fort William Henry, much less a thousand.

6
The Journey
11:12

T he group had been moving through the woods for over four hours. Heyward wanted to reach the fort before sundown, giving the girls time to bathe before dinner with their father. They urged their horses along, keeping them at a brisk walk.

Cora and Alice were doing fine, though their visages had become a bit frazzled, with tendrils of hair falling out from under their riding caps. They wore matching riding habits; Cora's was a deep red and Alice's a pale blue.

The major kept a conversation going with the ladies for the duration of the trip, barely even pausing to breathe. His questions were mostly directed at Alice, asking her about everything from her home in Scotland to her favorite pastimes and aspirations.

Heyward had turned to Alice to ask her what her favorite book was when a figure emerged from the woods. It was a woodsman, clothed in nothing but the same breech cloth as Magua. He was white, but his skin was tanned a light brown hue. He was a bear of a man, at least 6'5" in height and no less than 270 pounds, but all muscle. His light-brown hair reached his waist, with braids scattered among the tresses. He had a short, somewhat scruffy beard that he appeared to have trimmed, but had not had time to shave. There was a rifle strapped over his back, much longer than any Cora had ever seen.

Magua's eyes were trained forward, and he did not react to the newcomer's presence. Heyward guided his horse between the man and the ladies. The man didn't speak until he was right beside them, making Heyward uneasy. He had his hand on his pistol, ready to pull it out whenever necessary.

When the major didn't speak, Lieutenant Harchfield stepped forward. "Identify yourself before you come any closer, sir!"

The man chuckled.

"My name is Natty Bumppo, and I assure you I mean you no harm. I was hunting when I heard you passing by. Then I got to wondering where you all were headed?" The group continued walking, the man striding on beside them.

"That is none of your concern," Heyward said coldly, glaring at him. Mr. Bumppo held up his hands.

"As I said, I have no intention of bothering you; I am just curious."

"We are going to Fort William Henry," Cora responded.

Heyward sucked in a breath.

"Fort William Henry? The fort on the lake is nowhere near here. What trail are you following?" Bumppo asked, glancing at Magua every couple of seconds. The Huron's hand now rested on his tomahawk, but he kept his eyes trained forward.

"We are taking the back road, sir," Heyward responded.

"The back road? The trail you are referring to is five miles south of here," Bumppo said in a low voice. "Who is that guide up there? He doesn't look like an Iroquois."

"His name is Magua," Cora interjected, now eyeing the Wendat out in front of her. She lowered her voice. "Do you think he is leading us astray, sir?"

"He certainly is. I do not know where he is leading you, but it's not to the fort."

Heyward bit his lip. How was he to trust this random man who had appeared out of nowhere? He could be a French scout, or just a colonial trying to rob them. However, something didn't sit right in Heyward's stomach. Fort William Henry was northwest of Fort Edward, but they were traveling northeast. He hadn't noticed it until now because he was focused on talking to the ladies.

"You're right, sir. Thank you for pointing this out," Heyward responded. He nodded toward Magua, and Harchfield rode ahead of the group, bringing his horse to a slow walk beside Magua. Harchfield questioned Magua as to why they were headed in that direction.

"This is the trail," Magua responded, motioning at the trodden path they were walking on.

"We are not going the right way, Magua. Where are you taking us?" Harchfield demanded, jumping off his horse in front of the guide.

Magua gave Harchfield an annoyed look and tried to step past him. However, Harchfield stepped in front of the man again, his eyes narrowing. Suddenly, Magua thrust his blade into Harchfield's gut and dragged it up to the center of his chest. The man cried out but was quickly silenced when Magua pulled his knife out and slashed it across Harchfield's throat. Alice covered her eyes, screaming. Cora jumped off her horse's back and helped her sister onto the ground, and then dragged her off to the side of the clearing, picking up a large rock from the side of the path.

At the sound of the lady's cry, a dozen Wendat warriors emerged from the woods, shouting as they attacked. The men turned to fight. They all discharged their shots successfully, bringing down three of the natives, but those Wendats were replaced with their brethren, and the soldiers were forced to pull out their blades. They immediately engaged three of the attackers, trying to overpower them with brute force. Fortunately, no more than three of the Wendats had muskets.

Bennet rushed to stand between the ladies and the attacking Wendats. One of the Wendats saw this and leapt upon him. The boy, no more than eighteen, didn't last long against the grown native warrior. The Wendat had him on the ground with a knife in his chest within seconds.

At the sight of Bennet's body hitting the ground, Alice shrieked again and ran for the woods. The man who had just killed Bennet turned to chase after her, but Cora smashed the rock over his head. He fell, clutching the wound, which bled profusely. She leaned over his body, pulled his hatchet from his hand, and embedded it in his head. The man's blood splattered onto the skirt of Cora's dress.

Behind Alice, two other natives emerged from the woods. They didn't look like the Wendats who had been attacking them. Their hair was not slicked into a Mohawk; it was long and had small braids scattered throughout it.

Alice looked over her shoulder, hearing the men approaching, and shrieked. She rushed to Cora's side, and Cora raised the hatchet, ready to strike them. The men barely glanced at the ladies as they shot two Wendats and pulled out their blades, jumping on the nearest attackers and killing them within seconds.

Cora stood in front of her sister, holding up the hatchet, but she did not need to strike any others. Heyward, Hawkeye, and the Mohicans had killed all the remaining Wendats who attacked them.

Cora and Alice knelt beside Harchfield and Bennet, the former silently tearing up, the latter sobbing into her hands. Cora helped her sister to her feet, putting a hand on her shoulder.

"You were right, Mr. Bumppo! He was leading us astray! His men were waiting to attack us!" Cora said, bringing her sister forward to join the group of men. Hawkeye began checking the dead on the ground, and when he didn't see Magua's body, he quickly loaded his rifle.

"He's not dead, the Huron! He's around here somewhere!" Hawkeye said. The two natives who had joined them began looking around. The younger of the two saw Magua, who was crouching behind a bush, watching them, and he pointed him out to his older companion. Magua ran off into the woods, pursued by the two men.

Hawkeye turned to the group. Cora was talking with Heyward about how Bennet had died. Her sister was shaking, her hand covering her mouth. Her eyes were fixed on Bennet's body. Hawkeye approached the young woman gingerly.

"Are you alright, ma'am?" he asked. She flinched, but turned to face him, looking up at him with big eyes.

"Y-Yes, thank you. It's just... the man, she k-killed him," Alice stuttered, pointing at the man who had attacked her and her sister. The man's head was covered in blood, his face distorted by the split from the hatchet that Cora had wielded.

Hawkeye glanced at the body, and then at the elder sister, and finally noticed the blood covering her hands and the base of her dress, small speckles scattered on her face. His eyes widened.

"I... see," he responded.

Alice averted her eyes from the body and approached her sister, glancing back at the woodsman.

"You saved me, Cora," she said, throwing her arms around her sister, ignoring the blood from Cora's dress, which was now dirtying her own riding habit. The two embraced while Heyward introduced himself to Hawkeye.

"I'm Major Duncan Heyward. Pleased to make your acquaintance, Mr. Bumppo," Heyward nodded to the man.

"Hawkeye, call me Hawkeye. I only introduced myself as Bumppo before because I figured the Huron would recognize the name Hawkeye."

Heyward nodded.

"We surely would have perished if you and your *Indians* hadn't stepped in to save us."

"The Mohicans are not 'my' Indians. They are my family." Hawkeye gritted his teeth, proclaiming the truth of their relationship as his two companions emerged from the woods.

Upon seeing them, Hawkeye asked them in Algonquian if they had caught Magua. He dropped his head at his father's grim expression.

"Alright, Magua is still alive. And I guarantee he will be looking to find us again, with a new batch of men to attack us. So we'll need to get off this 'trail' and hole up somewhere safe for the night."

Heyward scoffed. "This is what we get for trusting an Indian."

Hawkeye turned to respond, but Cora beat him to it. "Sir, we were, in fact, saved by Indians," she snapped.

Uncas sucked in a quick breath.

Heyward opened his mouth to rebuke this, but before he could utter a response, a noise erupted from somewhere south of them. Someone was traveling toward them, and making an absolute ruckus. A man riding a horse emerged from the trees. He had long, dark brown hair and a full beard. He was wearing a tan trench coat that reached mid-calf and a typical colonial outfit below it, complete with overly tight, black, buckled shoes. His stockings were bright red, and he had large, knobby knees.

He entered the clearing, singing a psalm, pitch pipe in one hand and a small psalmody book in the other. The ladies smiled upon seeing such a display. The newcomer grinned when he saw the genteel ladies.

"Greetings, friends!" he said, bringing his horse to a stop. "My name is David Gamut, and I have been following you all, as I heard you were headed to Fort William Henry. I am to instruct the men there in psalmody," he said, making a small bow from atop his horse.

"Why would you just appear like that... making all that noise?!" Heyward demanded. "We could have shot you, not knowing who you were!"

"God watches over his servants, sir."

Heyward rolled his eyes, but didn't reply.

"If you were following us, perhaps you have heard that we are nowhere near the fort?" Cora responded, looking up at the man atop his horse.

His eyes widened. "Not near the fort? Why ever not, ma'am?"

"Our guide had ulterior motives and led us in the wrong direction, but have no fear. We are safe under the protection of Hawkeye and his friends..." Cora looked questioningly at the two men who stood beside Hawkeye.

"Uncas," the younger man said.

"...and Chingachgook," his father finished.

"Pleasant to meet all of you! And ladies, what are your names?" David questioned. The eldest Munro daughter answered for them, and Heyward added his own name after she had finished.

"Lovely! I hope you won't mind me singing for you as we journey together?"

"Together? When did I—" Heyward started.

"Of course, you may sing. You'll have to teach us some tunes on the way there!" Cora answered, cutting him off. Heyward glared at the older sister, who seemed insistent on contradicting everything he said.

Hawkeye smirked upon seeing this interaction but made no comment.

"We must get moving. The Huron will be back with more men, and if we stay here, we are asking to get killed," Chingachgook said. "We know a place. There is food and water there, and shel—"

"Now, listen!" Heyward interrupted. "We don't know you, so why would we follow you somewhere where you might just kill us?"

"Major Heyward, if they wanted us dead, why go to the trouble of killing our assailants?" Alice questioned quietly. Hawkeye bit his lip to stop the chuckle. When Heyward did not respond, he took a step forward.

"Look, Major, we have no ill intentions, but if we stay here, you will all die, Chingachgook is right, and there is no way that you will make it to the fort by nightfall since Magua led you so far astray," the scout said.

The major thought for a second before nodding.

"Very well, I suppose we could follow you. It seems we have no other choice."

"Great," Hawkeye said. "We cannot take the horses. They are much too easy to track."

Heyward opened his mouth, but held his tongue and gave another brisk nod. The ladies retrieved their belongings from the satchels hoisted over the horses' backs before the Mohicans slapped the animals' backsides, sending them running.

The group followed Hawkeye and the Mohicans away from the site of the attack.

7
Glen Falls

17:48

The canoe glided to a stop on the edge of the river. About one hundred yards away was a mountain, though it was so small that the word "mountain" didn't do it justice. The roar of water somewhere nearby also suggested the presence of a waterfall. Heyward exited and offered a hand to Alice to assist her out of the canoe. Alice murmured her thanks. Likewise, Uncas offered Cora his hand, which she accepted, smiling at him.

"Where are we going?" Alice whispered to her sister.

There was a small collection of large boulders in front of the mountain, but surely Chingachgook didn't mean for them to hide amongst the boulders?

They got closer and once they reached the boulders, Alice realized there was a cave entrance hidden behind them. It was smaller than a door, forcing Hawkeye to crouch and squeeze through the entrance.

The Mohicans led them all inside, and Alice took in her surroundings. The cave was somewhat large, tall enough that everyone, even the very tall Hawkeye, could stand without hitting their head. It also contained some furnishings. Alice didn't see any tables or chairs, but there were stands to put lit torches, blankets, a small pile of what appeared to be clothes, and simple dishes beside a hearth.

Hawkeye began working his hand drill to build a small fire. It was drafty in the cave, so Cora and Alice huddled together to keep warm. The psalmodist, David, was blowing a soft tune on his small, wooden flute, which soothed the ladies' nerves.

The fire Hawkeye built was starting to grow, so Alice and Cora moved toward it, rubbing their hands together. Soon, the others took seats around the fire too.

"How do you know of this place?" Alice asked Hawkeye.

"Ask my father, ma'am," Hawkeye said, nodding at Chingachgook.

Alice raised an eyebrow.

"Your father? Sir?"

Hawkeye smiled.

"Ma'am, I was born to an Englishman. No great colonel like yourself; not that it matters, as my parents died when I was three. Chingachgook rescued me from the burning cabin and took me in. He treated me like his own son, and his wife was like my mother," Hawkeye explained.

"And Uncas?" Cora asked, stealing a glance under her eyelashes.

"My brother was born around the time Chingachgook took me in. His mother died a few years after, killed by the same men who murdered my parents."

"I see," Cora said.

Hawkeye picked up some torches and set them alight, placing them in what appeared to be hitches made for torches.

"Shall I take first watch, Father?" Hawkeye asked. Chingachgook nodded, and Hawkeye went to exit the cave.

"A moment, Hawkeye..." Heyward asked, grabbing him by the arm. "What are we to do if we are attacked?"

Hawkeye pulled his arm out of the officer's hand.

"We can defend ourselves from the mouth of the cave. The boulders would act as cover for us. If need be, we can escape." Hawkeye gestured at Heyward to follow him to the back of the cave. There was a short corridor, no more than five feet tall, which led to a second room in the cave. Alice and Cora followed them as well.

Alice could make out the waterfall that they had been hearing this whole time through the back exit. The group could see that there was a walkway that went behind the falls. It led to the other side of the river, which must have been the escape that Hawkeye was referring to.

"This is Glen Waterfall," Hawkeye said, gesturing dramatically to the waterfall out in front of them. "The trip would not be easy for the ladies, so we will avoid it at all costs." Heyward nodded and returned inside to the cave. Alice stayed behind, admiring the beauty of Glen. Hawkeye remained by her side while the rest of the group went inside. He put a hand on her shoulder. She jumped, not expecting his touch, but didn't pull away.

"It's beautiful, isn't it?" he asked. She looked up at him with a meek smile, unsure how to put her thoughts into words. The waterfall fell right past the exit of the cave, crashing seventy feet below them. On the other side of the river were similar small mountains to the one they were in. Tall pine trees dotted the land between them. The river below snaked around the area, carving a path through the small mountains that decorated the landscape. The sky was light blue, almost white, and the first hints of a sunset were creeping up on the horizon.

"Magnificent. You live here?"

He chuckled.

"In a way. My family does not truly live anywhere. We are always moving. This is my favorite of our residences, because it feels like a home. But men of war are never stationary."

Alice nodded at this.

"True, it seems the only place my father has not been is home."

His lips thinned when he smiled, his eyebrows pulled to the middle.

"I'm sorry, Miss Alice, but I swear, you will see your father soon."

She gave him a smile at that and thanked him, putting a hand to her heart.

"I must stand guard now, I will see you safely into the cave with your sister, ma'am." He gently took her hand in his and led her into the cave, followed by Chingachgook.

The sisters sat against the rock wall, talking to each other in whispers. Heyward approached and sat beside them. "Are you ladies excited to see your father again?" he asked, his eyes fixed on Alice.

Alice looked at her hands, avoiding eye contact. "Why, of course, sir, it has been years since we've seen him."

"Have you lived here your whole life, Uncas?" Cora asked.

Uncas' head shot up at the use of his name. Cora's eyes were fixed on his face as he answered that he had.

"Where are your countrymen?"

"I have none, Miss Munro," he said in a solemn voice.

"None? Chingachgook, did Hawkeye not say you are a chief?"

Everyone in the cave turned to look at the sagamore. The man was around forty-five, but his eyes were old and war-torn. A handsome man, he had the same sharp cheekbones and dark brown eyes as Uncas. His hair was also long and scattered with braids, but unlike his son, Chingachgook's fringe was pulled out of his face and tied together in the back with a piece of leather. He had snakes tattooed above both eyebrows and several other tattoos lining his arms and chest.

Chingachgook's lips drew into a thin line. "I am, dear girl, but a chief of a dead tribe. My family, my people, are all gone."

"Gone? Why has this happened to your people?" Alice asked, sitting up away from the wall she had been lying against.

"There is no one reason," Uncas interjected. "When the white settlers came, they brought disease. The conflict with the French and the English drove a wedge between our people and the Delaware we lived with before, as we did not want to take sides."

"So, how many of you are left?" Alice asked, tears springing to her eyes.

"Just us, child," Chingachgook said, giving her a sorrowful smile.

Tears began to fall unbridled from Alice's eyes.

"That is horrible, I am so sorry, Chingachgook," she said, extending a hand and gently placing it on his shoulder. Chingachgook seemed taken aback by the sweet gesture but didn't pull away.

"Save your tears, child, nothing is to be done. I am on the hilltop, and I must go down into the valley and when Uncas follows in my footsteps, there ends the blood of my people, for my son is the last of the Mohicans," Chingachgook said, his voice filling with emotion. The cave was silent for a moment as Alice and her sister absorbed the truth.

It might have stayed silent forever if the psalmodist hadn't started blowing on his pitch pipe, readying the group for another hymn. The tune he played was sad and melodic.

Cora's gaze traveled to that of the young warrior, after hearing his story. He was such a brave young man, and so strong. She could not help but admire his countenance. He was a handsome man, with a sharp jawline and striking dark brown eyes. His long jet-black hair flowed down his back, with small braids scattered throughout it. He had a black line tattooed on his chin, running down from the center of his lips to the tip of his chin. Cora had always been taught not to ogle others, but it was impossible not to stare at such a perfect physique, as if carved by Michelangelo himself.

As she examined him, his eyes met hers, and they stared at each other for a second before she dropped her gaze. He stood up and crossed the cave to sit next to her. Heat rose on her face and she flushed bright red.

"Uncas..." she started, unsure of what to say to the young Mohican.

"Why do you come to these lands?" Uncas asked, handing her a water skin. Cora nodded her thanks.

"My father is in charge of Fort William Henry. My sister and I are to travel to meet him there," Cora explained. Uncas nodded in understanding. She took a small drink from the canteen.

"The fort on the lake is under siege," Uncas pushed. "Why do you come now?"

Cora almost choked on her water. *Why did General Webb not mention anything?*

"We didn't know the fort was under siege...Is it looking bad for my father?" Cora asked, reaching out to place a hand on Uncas' forearm.

"It is news. The siege has just started. As far as I understand, the general at Fort Edward has refused to send reinforcements, which makes your father's situation dire," Uncas said, unconsciously scooting closer to the young woman. "I'm sorry if this makes you nervous."

She smiled thinly. "No, please do not apologize, Uncas. I am glad I now know. I just hope my father is safe."

"I am sure he is, Cora," Uncas said, looking up to her eyes. Butterflies erupted in her belly at his use of her name. The young man had a silky, soothing voice and such a handsome countenance.

"Thank you, Uncas," she murmured, blushing.

"Where are you from?" Uncas asked.

"Scotland, it's part of Great Britain, across the ocean."

"Yes, the Scottish colonel is well loved among the colonials here," Uncas said. "But where did you grow up? Tell me about it."

"Dunbar, Scotland. I was three when Alice was born, and our mother died. Our father stayed with us for another five years and then the Army stationed him here in the Americas. I haven't seen him in almost a decade. We had a governess who hated us, so Alice and I were always close," Cora started.

"And your sister, you see her as a daughter, don't you?"

Cora smiled.

"I imagine I do a bit. She is both my best friend and the person I must protect above all," she explained. "Does Hawkeye view you in the same way?"

Uncas briefly glanced at the exit.

"I suppose he does."

"And what of you, Uncas, what was your childhood like?"

"My mother died when I was very young, and by that point, Hawkeye was already with us. He has always been like an older brother to me. When we each turned five, my father brought Hawkeye and me to a small school run by one of the mothers in the area. We both learned to speak English and some French there," Uncas said, glancing toward Hawkeye again.

"I see, that makes sense. So, what languages do you speak?"

"My language is Algonquian, the language of most Delaware. I speak English very well, almost fluently, I would say. I can pick up every couple of words in French, and I know a few Wyandot phrases from my times fighting the Hurons."

"That is very impressive! My sister and I only speak English fluently, though we both know some French and German. What else did you learn in that school?"

"Basic arithmetic, how to read and write, those kinds of lessons. The woman tried to teach us how to be 'proper' and follow her faith, but Hawkeye told her we had no interest in it," Uncas said with a faraway look.

Cora beamed.

"Is it typical for the natives here to speak English?"

"The natives that work with the English usually know a good amount of the language, and the same for the French, but they rarely take the time to become fluent," he explained.

Cora pursed her lips.

"And Magua?"

"To my knowledge, *Le Renard Subtil* spent years under your father, and I believe he spent most of his time just around white men, so he likely went years without speaking his language. Given that he is working with the French, I'd wager he speaks French as well, although it would be a marvel if he has picked it up so fast."

Cora nodded.

"You are the last of your tribe. Your people will die with you, but if there are other Delaware, why not partner with one of them?" Cora glanced up at him.

"Though there are Delaware women, none of them could truly save my tribe," Uncas started. "My father married for love, and I intend to follow his example. If I cannot find such a woman, I will never marry," he said. "And yourself? Why are you not married yet? I cannot imagine you lack suitors."

Cora laughed heartily. "I suppose that is true," she said smiling. "I guess I just haven't found the right man yet."

"I see. And what..." he hesitated. "...what is the right man?"

"I'm not exactly sure. I suppose just a man who treats me well, with whom I can laugh, and whom my father approves of," she said. After the last phrase, she shot him an awkward look before her eyes returned to the ground.

"And your father, what kind of man would he approve of?"

"He has always wanted only the best for me and my sister, but he has made it clear that as long as we love the man, and he is a good man, he will support it," she elaborated.

Uncas nodded, his lips curling into a small smile.

Uncas glanced briefly at her lips before returning his gaze to her light brown eyes. "You are as intelligent as you are beautiful, Cora," he said, giving her a shy smile. "Forgive me. I must bring my brother some food.

Cora sat there, as Uncas moved toward the exit of the cave, speechless at what he had just said. *How has this man come into my life today and made me question everything?*

Her cheeks were hot, and she felt something like butterflies fluttering around in her stomach. She was getting ahead of herself. They had only just met, and she was already having romantic thoughts about him! How quickly her mind seemed to fly.

Hawkeye stared out at the graying blue sky. The moon was rising above the river out in front of him. It was a beautiful night. He had spent many nights sitting out by these rocks, but he wasn't sure he'd ever seen a night like this.

It could have been that his exhaustion from fighting that day made it seem so beautiful, or maybe he just hadn't ever noticed because he was usually with his family, not sitting out here alone.

The blanket that covered the entrance was pushed aside, and his brother came out. His hands were shaking as he handed Hawkeye a wooden slab with venison on it; he almost dropped it. Hawkeye eyed his brother.

"What's wrong with you? Why're you shaking like a little pup?"

"Oh. I'm just not... used to being around... people."

Hawkeye chuckled.

"Ah, people, alright." He shooed his brother back inside.

People. Anyone with eyes can see it isn't people who are making Uncas so nervous. It's Cora.

The three men weren't often around women, so it made sense that Uncas was enamored with the first one he met. God knew he was.

Alice took small bites of the piece of venison that Chingachgook had given her. The old sachem was carving a design in the handle of his knife. Alice watched in wonder at the exact movements of his wrist, whittling away tiny shavings of wood at a time.

"How long have you been a sculptor?" Alice asked him.

Chingachgook smiled.

"A long time, Miss Alice."

"And do you keep your creations?" Alice asked, grinning.

"Not usually, ma'am. A man of the woods does not have space to carry such things around," Chingachgook explained.

Alice nodded, though her smile faded a little. "It is very sad that you must lose so many masterpieces..."

"Would you like one?" he asked, nodding toward the knife handle he was carving.

She shook her head. "You are most kind, but you need your knife, Chingachgook."

"I have others," he said, handing her the knife. There were small depictions of animals carved into the handle: a deer, a snake, a bird, and a butterfly. She twirled the knife in her hand, inspecting the designs he had carved into it.

"What do the animals mean?" She traced the snake with her index finger.

"They are my family, my dear," he said, smiling sadly at her.

"Your family?" Alice inspected the handle closer. "Oh, I see the hawk, that must be Hawkeye. But who are the others?"

"The deer is my son, Uncas—the Bounding Deer. The snake is me—the Great Serpent, and the butterfly... the butterfly is my wife, Apanii, the butterfly of my life," he explained.

Alice put a hand on his shoulder. "You must have loved her very much. I cannot accept this. You need this family portrait of sorts for yourself," she argued, trying to push the knife back into his hand.

"Nonsense, my child." Chingachgook pulled another other knife from his belt and showed her the same design etched into its handle. "I have plenty more; it has become an obsession of sorts."

"Why are you called the Great Serpent?" Alice asked.

"It has been said that I understand the winding of human nature, which winds much like a snake's body as it moves," he explained.

"He also strikes suddenly, causing quick deaths," Uncas said as he walked back into the cave. Alice nodded at this comment. She had seen the sagamore fight Magua and the Wendats, and he was much faster than any other man his age she knew, so the name seemed to do him justice.

"I see, that makes sense. I assume Bounding Deer refers to your speed, Uncas?" Alice asked. Uncas nodded. "And Hawkeye, that refers to his aim with the rifle?"

"That it does, ma'am," Chingachgook confirmed. "He was born Nathaniel Bumppo. Natty, if you will, but when he was eight or nine, he told me he did not like the name; that it was too hard to say. I let him choose a new one, and he decided on the nickname his friends from the school had taken to calling him: Hawkeye[1]."

"Now," he started, looking upon the younger sister. "You must be an artist yourself to appreciate my work so much. What do you do for art?"

The girl blushed and looked at her hands. "I... Well, I sing, if one can consider that art, and I write poetry."

"Sing? Well, you must sing for us, then!" Chingachgook said, smiling fondly at the young woman. Alice looked to her sister, as if for approval, and Cora nodded at her, grinning.

"Very well, what would you like to hear?" she asked.

"Whatever you like, sweet child," Chingachgook said, encouraging her.

Alice bit her lip. "I...well, I suppose I could sing something I wrote."

"Perfect! Entrance us, flower!" Cora called. Alice nodded, getting to her feet and standing before the group. She cleared her throat a little, worried that her voice might come out a croak.

"Through the trees and rolling green,
The wild winds moan and cry,
There's an unknown path, faintly seen,

---

1. In *The Deerslayer*, the first book chronologically in The Leatherstocking Tales, it is revealed that Hawkeye earned the name from a Huron he shot from a canoe. The backstory has been changed here because the events of *The Deerslayer* are not necessarily part of the backstory of the Mohicans.

Beneath the star-filled sky.
"For the night is dark and the enemies creep,
Through shadows from whom you canna hide,
We'll march ahead, no time to sleep,
Until in the forest we don't reside
"The forest where the old oaks stand,
And the river rushes by,
We must guard with a steady hand,
And utter our war cry,
"For the night is dark and the enemies creep,
Through shadows from whom you canna hide,
We'll march ahead, no time to sleep,
Until in the forest we don't reside
"With faith our shield and hope our guide,
We'll survive together, we shalln't divide,
For in each step, the future lies,
Beneath these star-filled skies.
When the enemy is gaining
And the light seems far away,
We canna forget our God who's reigning
Who, by our side, will always stay
"For the night is dark and the enemies creep,
Through shadows from whom you canna hide,
We'll march ahead, no time to sleep,
Until in the forest we don't reside
So let the winds blow and the rains descend,
We'll stay strong till journey's end,
Our enemies can never touch us,
For in the Lord we shall always trust."

The girl finished the song and looked around the cave, meeting Chingachgook's eyes finally.

"That was beautiful, child. You are a true songbird. You are Chulëntët,[2] a little bird, sweet girl," he said, smiling at her.

Alice blushed, unable to contain her grin.

Suddenly, a terrifying noise erupted from outside. Screeches tore through the night. The group all looked toward the entrance, frightened that whatever demon was making the ruckus would somehow enter the cave to devour them all.

Hawkeye rushed inside, looking around at the group with wild eyes.

"Never in my twenty-two years have I heard such a sound! What's happening?"

"Is it Indians?" Alice asked.

"No, Miss Alice," Hawkeye replied.

"Then some terrible animal, a bobcat or wolf, or something?" Cora suggested.

"Aye, it's an animal. But what animal? I've never heard such hellish, unearthly sounds all my life," Hawkeye said.

"We must investigate!" Heyward moved toward the mouth of the cave. Uncas and Hawkeye followed him, moving out into the night, hearing the noises without the distortion of the cave.

"Oh, it's the horses," Heyward said, almost instantly.

"Horses? I'll have to take your word for that, sir. No horse I've ever heard sounded like that," Hawkeye replied.

---

2. Chulëntët means "little bird" in Lenape.

"I've heard the noise in battle; it's the sound of a horse that is hurt or scared," Heyward elaborated. As he explained this, howls emerged from the woods where the horses were tethered.

"I see," Hawkeye said, and the three men entered the cave again to explain the noises to the rest of the group.

"What was it?" Cora asked, addressing Uncas directly.

"The horses, ma'am. We think wolves got them."

"Horses? That was horses?" Alice asked, frowning.

"It's the cave, Miss Alice. It plays tricks with sounds from outside," Hawkeye said. Alice nodded.

The group gathered around the fire that Uncas had made. Chingachgook began slicing pieces of meat off the cooked carcass of the deer he had killed that morning. He handed them out to everyone. The ladies thanked him graciously before huddling together.

"And now that we have received food, may we thank the Lord for being so generous to us!" David said, jumping to his feet and putting the pitch pipe to his lips. He blew a clear note and then announced that they would be singing Psalm 116.

The group all began singing, which calmed their nerves. However, the imminent threat of the Wendats was constant, especially among the three men, who tossed glances at the entrance every few minutes.

Hawkeye was still standing guard outside, but the rest remained there for some time, conversing with each other, and telling anecdotes. Cora sat beside the young Mohican, and the two continued their conversation from earlier.

"In Scotland, how did you and Miss Alice entertain yourselves?" Uncas asked, turning to look at her.

"We did quite a few things. My sister finds the most joy in playing instruments, the harp most of all," Cora started, glancing at her sister. "She has always been a very talented musician. Maybe someday you will have the opportunity to hear her play."

"She plays as well? She has such a beautiful voice. Adding an instrument must make it perfect," he said. "And yourself?"

"I enjoy reading, and my father instilled in me a love for hunting and shooting."

"Hunting? This is allowed for women? I thought that the white men do not like their women being physical," Uncas said, raising an eyebrow.

"This is true," Cora admitted. "If my father were not a lieutenant colonel, I'm sure I would not have been allowed to pursue such interests. But his influence has helped."

"That is fortunate, I suppose," Uncas responded, smiling. "And what did you hunt? Hinds and wolves?"

Cora chuckled.

"No, no. Nothing that big. Just pigeons, rabbits, foxes, those sorts of things."

"Ah, I see. But still, a huntress is a huntress," he said. Her eyes were bright as she smiled at him.

"And what books do you read?"

"Adventure stories, mostly," she said. "Stories that feel like our adventure right now."

"And are you enjoying this adventure?"

"Of course! I mean, it's certainly been dangerous, and a part of me is constantly worried that something bad will happen, or that my dear sister will be harmed. But running around the woods and traversing the river in canoes is so invigorating, and I've had the opportunity to meet you and your family. You are all such good people," she said, looking over at Chingachgook briefly.

"I appreciate you saying that, Cora," Uncas said. Cora grinned at him, feeling the butterflies from before taking flight.

"Of course, Uncas!" she exclaimed. "And what do you do for entertainment?"

"There is little time for entertainment on the frontier. The three of us spend our days hunting game for our meals. My brother and I jest a lot, but we don't have books to read," Uncas started. Cora blushed, embarrassed to have brought this up if he did not have any experience with it.

"I'm sorry—"

"Don't be! We have fun, just in a different way to you and your family. My brother and I race and wrestle a lot. We swim in the Hudson. We make fun out of our situations, like anyone would, I suppose."

"I see." Cora got a playful look in her eyes. "And who wins?"

Uncas chortled. "I am faster; the Bounding Deer, but Hawkeye is stronger."

"That makes sense," she said. She paused, biting her lip. "Growing up was rather odd for Alice and I. Not many knew about our father, as he ensured that only those he could trust did, but our... my heritage is not that of a typical Scottish woman..." Cora started, knowing if she was to think of this man in a romantic way at all, he would need to know about her background.

Uncas' eyebrow quirked. "What do you mean?"

"My mother was the descendant of a black slave. Her grandmother's mother was a slave. My blood is, in the view of many, tainted. I have no issue with this, but the reason I'm sure I'll never find a partner is that no 'good gentleman'...". she practically spat the words. "...would ever take into his home a woman descended from someone black," she said, looking at her hands, unable to meet Uncas' eyes, for fear of what she could find there. Cora felt no embarrassment or guilt for her heritage, but she knew it would disgust most men.

Uncas put his hand under her chin gently and raised her head, bringing her eyes to his own. "Cora, any man who would think any differently about you or your sister has neither heart nor brains."

She laughed at this, holding her stomach to try and calm herself. Some small part of her felt relieved that he said so, but she mentally chided herself. *How could someone like Uncas, who knows how ridiculous those prejudices are, feel any differently?*

"And your hair," she continued. "Do you all braid each other's hair or is this something you've learned to do on your own?"

He smiled at the question.

"It's very simple, really. We bathe and swim in the river as often as we can, and braiding is just something we started to pass the time while our hair dried," he explained.

"I see. It's very nice that you're able to keep yourselves so clean. I assume that is one of the reasons you choose to live beside the river and waterfall?"

"It is, but also to have a water source so close to where we live. Would you like braids?" he asked. Her eyes brightened, and she nodded, turning so that he could reach her hair.

Uncas picked up a small section of her loose, curly hair and began weaving the strands together to form a small braid. He did this several times, always careful not to tug on her hair.

Cora's breath caught in her throat as his hand grazed her neck when he reached for another section of her hair. The juxtaposition between Uncas' ferocious fighting against the Wendats and his gentle, braiding hands was odd but also strangely soothing.

"Done," he said in her ear.

She turned back to look at him, her lips pulled into a grin.

"How do I look?" she asked. Cora felt the back of her head with her hand, running her fingers over a braid.

"Breathtaking," he said instantly, not giving his brain time to filter itself. "Yet it is incomplete…"

Her eyebrows furrowed. "What do you mean?"

"Just give me a second." Uncas got to his feet and exited the cave.

He soon returned, holding a flower in his hand. It was a bright red carnation. He pulled his knife from his belt and cut down the stem before adding it to Cora's hair, letting the stem sit in one of the braids.

"Now you look perfect," he said.

Cora felt her cheeks flush a bright red, and she thanked him, unable to stop herself from beaming.

"I um…I really enjoy your conversation, Uncas. I don't believe I've ever met someone with such an ability to be caring and gentle while still being so strong." No man had ever made her this nervous before. She laughed awkwardly, unsure of what to say. Uncas smiled, chuckling along with her.

"I appreciate you saying so, Cora. The feeling is mutual."

Her laugh devolved into a yawn, and she stretched her arms above her head. When she finished, Uncas put a hand on hers.

"You should get some sleep, Cora," he said, his eyes creasing in the corners. She nodded, knowing he was right. He dipped his head down and laid a gentle kiss on her hand. Cora's heart jumped, and she smiled up at him, her heart racing.

"Thank you, Uncas." The young Mohican nodded and left her side, making his way to his brother. Cora rose to her feet and approached the corner where Chingachgook had spread a pile of hay for her and Alice to sleep on.

The sisters huddled next to each other, Cora rubbing Alice's hand gently to calm her. They stayed like that for some time. Cora's eyes were heavy and she soon fell asleep.

Alice's head raced with her thoughts, never able to focus on one thing for more than a few seconds. After a few hours had passed, she slowly rose from her sister's side, taking care not to wake her, and approached the entrance to the cave, intent on looking at the stars to calm her thoughts.

As she crossed the threshold of the cave, she emerged beside Hawkeye, who had been keeping guard for the last two hours.

"Can't sleep, Miss Alice?" he asked her, his eyes dancing in the moonlight.

She gave a small smile. "I can't imagine I'd be able to, even with the exertions of the journey. I am frightened, Mr. Hawkeye."

He chuckled at this. "You need not call me 'Mr. Hawkeye', ma'am, I'm just Hawkeye, no gentleman."

"Titles and ranks don't make gentlemen. This is one thing I've learned, but if you wish for me to call you Hawkeye, I will. But you must call me Alice.

"There are no titles in the wilderness, I suppose. The Hurons don't care if you're a peasant or a duke when they scalp you," Hawkeye said.

"That's true." Alice bit her lip, unsure how to progress the conversation.

"And how do you find the sky tonight, Hawkeye?"

"It is beautiful. Every night here is more stunning than the last." He stared up at the vast openness about them, then looked down at the angelic face of the youngest Munro daughter. "And what do you think of it, Alice?" She blushed under his gaze.

"The skies in Scotland are just as beautiful, but there is something different about the air here, the smell of the pine trees, and the gentle breeze. It's all so calming," she said, breathing it in through her nose.

It seemed the forest was beginning to grow on the gentle girl. Hawkeye observed her with a grin hidden by the dark of the night. She was beautiful, but in a different way than her sister. Alice's features were soft, and her pale blonde hair didn't contrast as sharply with her light skin as her sister's did. And whereas Cora was no taller than 5'3" and had a shapely body, Alice was closer to 5'8" and very slim. There were also freckles sprinkled over the lady's nose and cheeks.

"I agree," he said.

A noise came from out in the woods, not loud and not sudden, but Alice gasped and grabbed Hawkeye's arm. The scout instantly moved between her and the forest.

"You should head inside, Alice. Try and get some sleep if you can," he said, looking at her over his shoulder. She took a step back.

"Are we in danger?" she asked, eyeing the woods cautiously.

He shook his head. "I'm sure it was nothing more than a coyote. I will let you all know if there is danger."

"Very well, stay safe, Hawkeye." The young woman returned to her sister, where she also eventually fell asleep.

4 August 1757

8
The Dispatch
00:07

T he portrait hanging above the bookshelf seemed to be frowning at General Webb. He gazed at the clock on the wall and realized that he had been working for far too long. Not just that day, either. He had awoken at 04:30 and worked nonstop, barely allowing himself time for a meal or a trip to his chamber pot, until 22:30.

Webb yawned and turned to the plate of food that he had received four hours earlier. The man was nearing eighty, and he was much too old to be dealing with work so late in the day. However, retirement wasn't an option. He would never leave the service until this God-forsaken war was over and the French agreed to stay in Canada.

A loud rap sounded on his office door, and it shook. Webb groaned and called for the knocker to him in. His secretary, Sergeant Boyd, entered the room and removed his hat, bowing.

"Good evening, General Webb!"

Webb nodded in acknowledgment.

"Good evening, Sergeant. I trust you have a good reason for barging into my office so late at night?" He raised an eyebrow at the man.

"Forgive me, sir. We just received a dispatch from Fort William Henry, and the runner informed us that it was urgent," Boyd said, looking at the ground as he pulled out the folded-up parchment.

"Henry? What does Munro want at this late hour?" Webb asked, pulling the paper out of Boyd's hand. He examined the letter, and sure enough, it was Munro's seal. Webb could tell the paper had been sealed in a hurry; the wax was completely off center, and it had run down the paper, which meant Munro hadn't even let it fully dry before sending out the runner.

He ripped the seal in half and consumed the contents of the letter. He rolled his eyes after finishing it and handed it to the sergeant to read. Boyd's eyes flew across the page and then he looked up to meet Webb's gaze.

"Well, what do you think, Sergeant? What would you do in my situation?"

Boyd bit his lip.

"Well, sir, surely he must be mistaken? Montcalm wouldn't come out of Canada, not right now," he said, eyeing the paper once again.

"You would think that, but I know Montcalm. He would. Munro is requesting men, but I have none to give him. Henry is going to fall, and Montcalm will turn on us when it does. It is better for us to keep our strength and then wait for Munro's men to join us here and take Montcalm on as a joint force," Webb said.

"But...Sorry, never mind me, sir," Boyd started before trailing off and looking down at his hands.

"I assume you were going to suggest that sending men would allow us to keep the fort and defeat them now, but you are wrong. We wouldn't be able to send enough troops to defeat Montcalm while also protecting our own fort. Sure, Montcalm is only now coming out of Canada, but he has Indian allies here that would attack us should we make ourselves so vulnerable."

Sergeant Boyd nodded. "Understood. So you will reply tonight, sir?"

"No, bring me my stationery tomorrow morning at 0500 and we will get the dispatch out before dawn."

"Very well, sir, have a good night!" Boyd bowed to the general and left the office.

Webb ascended the stairs to his bedroom.

9
Morning

06:29

C ora was the first to wake. She emerged from under the blanket
she had used, approaching Hawkeye and Uncas. The brothers
sat by the burning coals of the fireplace, discussing the current situation with the ladies and the fort under siege.

"Good morning, gentlemen." Cora put a hand to her mouth to
mask a yawn. "How did you sleep?" she asked, her eyes drawn to the
younger brother.

"Well, but very little, I stood guard twice." Uncas handed her a
wooden plate of sorts that had an array of nuts and berries as well as
some slices of salmon. She nodded her thanks to him. "I apologize for
not having more meat; there is only so much food we can cook while
keeping the fires low."

"No need for apologies, Uncas. I am very grateful that we have
food. My sister and I expected to fast on our journey. We are more
than appreciative that you were able to provide anything at all!" she
reassured him.

He gave her a smile as he ate his own small portion of salmon and
raspberries.

Alice rose from her own spot, putting a hand to her temple. Heyward was instantly at her side, helping her across the cave to where the

rest were sitting. She accepted his help, and the two sat beside each other. Uncas offered them both their own slabs of food, which they accepted.

"Has Chingachgook eaten?" Alice questioned, looking toward the entrance to the cave, where she could just make out the figure of the older Mohican. Hawkeye smiled.

"I appreciate your concern for our father. He will join us in a minute," Hawkeye assured her. Alice nodded. And sure enough, *Le Gros Serpent* entered the cave a minute later, accepting food from his son.

"We must now begin the journey to your father," Chingachgook said. He turned to David. "As calming as your tunes are, we cannot have psalmody until we know we are safe," he said.

"No trouble, friend. I understand."

The group began collecting all their things and readying themselves to leave. Cora noticed her sister staring warily at the exit to the cave. She reached her hand out and held Alice's hand.

"It's alright, flower, the Mohicans will protect us."

Alice nodded, giving her sister a weak smile.

"Is everyone ready to embark?" Chingachgook questioned. They all nodded and followed his lead, ducking out of the cave.

Cora drank in the world outside the cave. There was a lush forest across the river. She could hear the waterfall on the other side of the cave from here. Aside from the running water, it was quiet.

BANG!

David's body slammed into the rock behind him, blood flowing from the back of his head. Alice screamed and Cora pulled her down, taking cover behind the rocks.

Uncas lowered the psalmodist to the ground with them, throwing his head to David's chest.

"He's alive!"

"Help me get him inside! The ladies will tend to the wound!" Hawkeye urged, and the brothers heaved David's limp body back into the cave they had just left. The ladies hurried in behind them, crouching low.

The men began shooting at the Wendats across the river who were attacking. They had the advantage of having rifles, while the Wendats mostly carried cheap muskets.

"How many are there?" Heyward questioned. "I can see at least a dozen."

"Two scores, at least." Chingachgook loaded his rifle, took aim, and fired, felling a Wendat who had risen too high from behind his cover.

"What do we do if they rush us? There's only four of us!" Heyward demanded.

"The river will slow them down to be sure, but if they all decided to rush us at once, I doubt we'd be able to keep them off," Chingachgook said.

Hawkeye, Uncas, and Cora joined them from the cave.

"Alice is tending to David's wound, so I will load your rifles for you." Cora took the rifle that Chingachgook had just discharged, then handed him one of the muskets they had captured from the Wendats killed in the ambush.

Chingachgook smirked at this and gave his son a grin. Uncas chuckled to himself and began to shoot. In the minutes that followed, Cora was constantly reloading someone's gun and handing it off to one of the men. The rocks they hid behind provided excellent cover, and aside from David, none of them were so much as grazed by the Wendats' bullets. Then the Wendats began to rush them.

Fifteen Wendats rushed across the river, shouting as they ran. They each fired their muskets before slinging them over their shoulders and pulling out their hatchets and knives. Hawkeye, Uncas, Heyward, and Chingachgook fired in response, then handed their weapons back to Cora for reloading.

Cora's fingers worked quickly, pouring powder in the pan of the musket she worked on.

The Mohicans and Hawkeye all pulled their bows from their backs and picked off the warriors advancing on them.

"I've got the front one!" Uncas shouted above the ruckus. His arrow coursed through the air, impaling the approaching Wendat in the neck.

Hawkeye was less successful; his arrow hit a Wendat in the arm. The man screamed, but kept running, snapping off the length of the arrow.

The Wendats leapt over the rocks, connecting with the four men, who dropped their bows and pulled out their knives and hatchets.

One of them threw himself at Uncas, who instantly sidestepped the attack and thrust his knife into the man's side. Hawkeye went on the offensive, grabbing his attacker by the wrist. He twisted him to face away from him, overpowered him, and dragged his knife across the man's throat. Shoving the man's limp body, he wiped the blood off his hands.

Chingachgook bashed the Wendats on the ground with his club before they even knew he was there. Suddenly, the final man lunged at Cora, grabbing her by the hair. She shrieked. Uncas turned at the sound and rushed to protect the dark-haired daughter, but found the man already lying at her feet, a knife embedded firmly in his heart.

He was staring at her unabashedly when his brother yanked him down behind the rock again. There were still around twenty Wendats on the other side of the river, firing at the group.

"I'm going to go check on David," Cora said. She kept her head low, crawling over toward the entrance.

BANG!

A bullet hit the rock face millimeters from her head, spraying small chunks of rock everywhere. Cora cried out and clutched at her eye.

Uncas instantly pulled her toward him.

"Are you alright?" he asked, inspecting her face for wounds.

She dabbed at her eye with her sleeve. "Yes. It was just the dust."

He nodded and helped her through the entrance of the cave before turning back to the other men.

"That shot came from above!" Hawkeye said, now scanning the surrounding trees. "Find the shooter!"

The men all scanned the thick foliage until Hawkeye saw the man, his legs straddling a large branch. He was pressing the ramrod down the length of the barrel, almost finished reloading.

Hawkeye raised his rifle and breathed in as he aimed. The report of his shot echoed around the hills. The Wendat's body toppled over as he fell from the branch he had been perched on. However, he managed to get a grip on a lower one that hung over the river.

"Finish him, Hawkeye!" Heyward demanded.

Hawkeye frowned. "He's been shot, Major. Why would I shoot him again?"

"He's not dead! Finish him, as you would a stag," Heyward persisted.

"He's not a stag, and we haven't the lead nor the powder for it!" Hawkeye argued.

"Shoot him!"

"No!"

"I will shoot him if you do not, and you have the better shot…"

"It's not just your own scalp that hangs in the balance, Major, but the ladies' as well!"

"I am a man of honor; I will not let a man suffer so!" Heyward insisted.

Hawkeye huffed at the foolish man's stubbornness.

"Very well!" He raised his now-loaded rifle to his eye and fired, dropping the man into the river. Then he turned on Heyward. "That was the action of a boy; we do not have enough powder to waste on your honor!"

Heyward scowled, but he did not protest further.

"Everyone, empty your powder horns into mine, so that we may see how many shots we have left!" Hawkeye instructed. They all did as commanded, and Hawkeye emptied the contents into his own powder horn.

"They'll send another man up that tree, and if I don't shoot him, they'll know our position. At that point, it's only a matter of time before the rest rush us."

10
Departure

08:12

Everyone except Hawkeye retreated into the cave. He watched the ladies throwing furtive glances over their shoulders as he sat outside, waiting to see if any other Wendats decided to climb the tree.

"Ladies, may I suggest you retire to the back of the cave?" Major Heyward urged. "We will be discussing harsh topics, and I wouldn't want to offend your delicate natures."

Cora's eyebrows raised.

"We will stay, sir. Our delicate natures can withstand the conversation that will determine our fate."

"Very well," Heyward said, exasperated.

"We cannot escape, ladies," Hawkeye said as he walked back into the cave, having rid the Wendats of their climbing companion. "There are so many Hurons, we'd never be able to get out of here, save swimming the river, and you ladies would never be able to stay afloat in those dresses,"

"And we can't swim," Alice added.

Hawkeye's eyebrows jumped.

"Ah, yes, so that escape route is totally out."

"But you men could; you could swim out and escape," Cora suggested. "Hawkeye, you've all done far too much for us; we cannot allow you to become more involved in our troubles."

"What do you mean, Miss Munro? You cannot be suggesting what I think you are," Hawkeye said.

"Yes, there is a way to escape; there is no reason for you all to stay here and die!"

"But ma'am! Would you have us abandon you?" Hawkeye demanded, folding his arms.

"Chingachgook," Cora said, turning to the sagamore. "We are women, the daughters of a lieutenant colonel. Would Magua risk killing such a prize?"

"No, my dear. He would take you to sell to the French, but would you have us give you to them?"

"This is true," Hawkeye interjected. "And they'd leave David alive as well; they wouldn't kill a madman." He glanced over at the psalmodist.

David snorted. "A madman? The only thing I am mad for is my Lord, sir." He put his hand to his heart.

The woodsman chuckled at this, patting him on the back.

"Gentlemen," Cora continued. "The rest of you must go. Alice, David, and I will stay here. If you reach my father, you may bring help for us; we may be saved."

"And what would I say to the colonel?" Hawkeye ran a hand through his hair. "Tell him I left his daughters in the middle of the woods, to be taken by hostile men with intentions to sell them for ransom?"

"My father would understand this if you explained it, especially if you told him it was my idea," Cora argued.

"She's right, Hawkeye," Alice said, taking a step toward him. His eyes softened as he looked down at the younger sister.

"Well…" Hawkeye hesitated. He turned to Chingachgook. "What say you, Father? What of Miss Munro's plan?"

Chingachgook gave the woman a small, almost proud smile. He got to his feet and stepped toward the lady, taking her hand in his and giving it a gentle kiss.

"My dear, you are incredibly brave and you have the soul of a Mohican. You are a wolf, my dear, with equal intelligence, bravery, and beauty. You shall be Tëmetët,[1] for your intelligence may save us yet," he said.

Cora gave him a weak smile.

"Ladies," Hawkeye interjected. "If they take you, you need to do what they tell you. Do not fight them. They likely won't kill you. They will want you for the profits, but once you become more work than you are worth they may still kill you."

"We understand," Cora said.

"Very well," Major Heyward said. "You must all be off then." He nodded toward Hawkeye and the Mohicans.

Cora shook her head. "And yourself, Major. The Hurons will not kill us, but you will not be spared."

"I will not leave, Miss Munro. My life has already been purchased by my king to be given in his service. I am to protect you, or die trying," he said, his chin raised.

For once Hawkeye felt some semblance of respect for the man. He might have been a prejudiced, arrogant prick, but he was brave.

"Then we must be going," Hawkeye said, giving Major Heyward a respectful nod. The group followed him to the back of the cave. They all squatted into the small part of the cave that was hidden.

---

1. Tëmetët means "little wolf" in Lenape.

Hawkeye began letting down a long rawhide rope so he, Uncas, and Chingachgook would have a way to climb down.

"When we leave, put that brushwood in the entrance, and stay down. Stay quiet. If you do that, they may not find you, and we may yet save you," Hawkeye said, nodding toward the pile of brushwood in the corner. He looked at the younger Miss Munro. "I will see you again."

Alice swallowed, nodding.

Hawkeye began lowering himself down the rope, his father following him. However, Uncas lingered, his gaze still on the dark-haired daughter.

"I will stay," Uncas said, taking Cora's hand in his own.

Her face flushed as she looked up into his earthy brown eyes. She brought her other hand up, taking his other hand in hers.

"No, Uncas, you will go. To stay would be to die, and I could not live with myself if you died on my account. You will live, and I will see you again," she urged.

He nodded and turned to leave before she spun him around again, got up onto her tiptoes, and laid a small kiss on his cheek. "I will not forget that you wanted to stay."

His hand went up to feel the remnants of her kiss as he approached the edge of the cliff to climb down after his family.

"I will return," he promised, holding eye contact with the dark-haired sister. The last thing he saw before the descent was Cora's gaze, still trained on him.

II
Magua
08:20

The ladies retreated to the corner of the cave, arms wrapped around each other as they waited for the inevitable. Alice's face was pressed to her sister's bosom, and a now conscious David thumbed through his psalm book, murmuring the psalms to himself.

Loud shouts and cries sounded outside; Magua's men had reached the cave. The sisters cringed as they heard the shouts echoing through the cave. Heyward stood at the ready, sword raised, eyes fixed on the small entrance.

The Wendats in the other section of the cave were conversing with each other in Wyandot, so none of their conversation was intelligible to the group.

Cora's eyes were trained on the bush that covered the entrance. She listened to the Wendats in the other section of the cave rummaging through the humble furnishings of the Mohicans and throwing brush out of their way, unintentionally adding more protection to the shield.

The four of them were so focused on the connector of the caves that they did not hear the rustling of leaves behind them. Alice, whose head now rested on her sister's shoulder, felt the hair on the back of her neck stand on edge. She open her eyes, raising her head to see the figure of Magua standing in the back of the cave.

Her face went white and she screamed, upon seeing the face of the man who had led them so astray.

Her sister spun around and made eye contact with the interloper.

"Magua!" Cora shouted, moving to stand in between her sister and the man, keeping Alice away from the villain.

His lip curled into a smirk.

"So clever, hiding back here."

She didn't respond, only watched him, her mouth falling open. He called out to his comrades, and they all began pulling aside the brush.

Heyward pushed the women behind him, holding up his sword.

"Stay back, heathen."

Magua's expression was almost bored.

"There are ten of my men in the main section of the cave, and the only thing keeping them from killing you is me. Put down your sword, fool."

"Please do what he says, Major," Alice said, her voice breaking.

Heyward's eyes flashed, but he eventually lowered his weapon. Seeing his surrender, Magua stepped in toward him and took the sword from his hand. He called out to his friends in the rest of the cave and they began pulling the brush aside, revealing the connection between the rooms. Magua led Heyward through first, shoving him to the ground in the middle of his men.

"Do what you will, but leave him alive," he instructed in Wyandot.

Magua gestured for the ladies to enter the larger portion of the cave and David followed them, pressing a kerchief to his head and murmuring to himself. The Wendats went at Heyward, a swarm of punches and kicks that the British officer was barely able to fend off.

"Get your dogs off me!" he yelled.

Magua leaned against the wall of the cave, emotionless, ignoring Heyward's shouts. Heyward was a good fighter, even landing a few punches on his attackers, but there were too many of them, and he was quickly bloodied and bruised.

Magua raised his hand. "Alright, that's enough."

The men pulled away, leaving the man on his hands and knees, shooting daggers at Magua.

The ladies had sat down and were now holding each other tight, waiting to see what Magua would do next.

Magua approached Heyward and grabbed him by his overcoat, pulling him to his feet with ease and shoving him against the wall.

"Where is *La Longue Carabine*?" he demanded.

Heyward scowled, his face contorted in pain and anger.

"He's gone, Magua. Gone to where you may not reach him!"

"And where might that be, Major? You think I will not reach him? Magua can reach anything." Magua pulled his own knife out and held it to Duncan's face.

"He escaped, him and the Mohicans," Heyward said, his eyes shifting to Alice, who grimaced.

Magua laughed heartily.

"Escaped? And how did he do that? We've been watching every bit of this cave. The only way he could have gotten out was if he jumped..." Magua's eyes widened, his face rippling with anger. Then he took a deep breath, calming himself. "No matter! We will find them, and I will punish him for coming up with such a plan."

"You will do no such thing," Cora said, lifting her head. "The idea was mine, not his, so you may leave Hawkeye out of this!"

Magua released Heyward, letting him fall to the ground. He turned to face the dark-haired sister.

"Does the lady wish that I punish her instead?" Magua asked, his eyebrows rising.

Cora bit her lip, but remained silent.

"Make yourselves comfortable," he said with a small chuckle as he left the cave.

Outside, Magua conversed with Sayowahes,[1] sitting beside the rocks that the Mohicans had used for cover just half an hour earlier. Magua's lips were drawn in a thin line; his brain ached.

"What are you thinking, my brother?" Sayowahes asked in Wyandot.

"I've worked for a decade to get my revenge, and now it is within grasp, and I am unsure how to take it." Magua looked up at his friend.

"Your mind has been changed?"

"I hate him, with so much of my soul, but I can't bring myself...I just c-can't..." Magua stuttered, trying to articulate his thoughts.

Sayowahes smiled. "I understand, Magua. You didn't expect to like her."

Magua gave him with a helpless look.

Sayowahes was beginning to chuckle, and Magua began swatting at him to get him to shut up, when one of his men called his name.

Hatirontha[2] stepped out of the cave, glancing back over his shoulder before stepping toward his chief.

"Magua, the officer wants to talk."

---

1. The name Sayowahes means "He goes to seize them" in Wyandot.

2. The name Hatirontha means "He attracts" in Wyandot.

Rolling his eyes, Magua got to his feet, and made his way into the cave to see Heyward still standing in front of the ladies, his arms crossed, staring at the entrance expectantly.

"I will listen now," Magua said, glaring.

"What is your plan, Magua? Will you bring us to General Montcalm and sell us for ransom?" Heyward demanded.

Shrugging, Magua leaned against the wall, his arms folded in front of him.

"Would it not be smarter to bring them to their father and ask him for ransom? Would the father of such ladies not pay more than the man besieging his fort? The colonel would never give up his fort to save his daughters from the French prisons, and Montcalm knows that."

How would this arrogant twat have any clue what the French father knows and doesn't know?

"I promise that if you were to return the colonel's daughters to him, he would be encouraged to provide you with whatever financial reward you require: guns, ammo, spirits, anything!"

Magua's eyebrow quirked upward. He was tickled that the major assumed he was concerned with simple material things like guns, which, knowing Colonel Munro, would undoubtedly be old and rusty.

"It is an attractive offer," Magua said before exiting the cave again to sit with Sayowahes.

He kept his ear tuned into what was said inside the cave, curious how they would react.

"Well, it seems as if he may take that offer," the major said. Magua could practically see the man grinning, satisfied with himself.

"Duncan, you've been so clever!" the younger sister said.

Magua leaned against the side of the rock, listening, making eye contact and smirking at Sayowahes. Inside the cave, the psalmodist started singing hymns in a loud, boisterous voice.

12
Finding the Fort

08:45

U ncas caught hold of a stray branch that extended over the river, then pulled himself onto the wet earth that bordered the water. He had managed to keep a hold of his rifle and bow, despite the water crashing down on him at the bottom of the falls; however, he had lost his hatchet, knife, and powder horn.

With no way of knowing where his family might have washed up, Uncas began down the length of the river, scanning the water and riverbank for any sign of his brother or father.

His search ended when he made out the faint print of a moccasin on the wet riverbank. The walker had attempted to hide his trail by walking in the water, but the river had receded here, and Uncas could still make out the footprints in the mud. His father would never be so careless. Uncas began running in the direction that Hawkeye had taken.

After running hard for nearly five minutes Uncas finally caught up with his brother, who was with his father. The three of them headed straight for Fort William Henry, which was around four hours away.

They heard the fort before they saw it. Below them, the siege guns fired, and the canons of the fort boomed in retaliation. Smoke rose above the trees in the direction of the lake.

"Keep your heads down, we'll be in sight by now, I'm sure," Hawkeye said.

Around six thousand French troops besieged the fort and nearly two thousand natives fought with them. The natives would be scouring the woods to ensure that no runners from Edwards could get through.

Suddenly, Hawkeye ducked behind a tree. He looked over at his brother and father, who had taken cover opposite him, and motioned with his head. Uncas nodded, catching sight of the Wendat coming up the hill toward them.

Hawkeye jumped out from behind the tree and the Wendat turned on him, his eyes bulging in shock. He began to raise his gun, but Uncas' arrow was already protruding from his neck before he could ever point the musket at Hawkeye. Uncas swiftly collected his arrow, and they moved closer to the fort.

Uncas had never seen a fort under siege before, but it was everything he had imagined it to be: impossibly loud, frantic, and chaotic, and hardly anything was visible through the smoke of the cannons and the fog from the lake.

He gazed out at the expanse before him from the top of the hill. The French pickets stretched out around the fort, blocking anyone from getting in or out. Uncas realized they would never get in, not now, and certainly not when they were escorting the women here. The only way to make it through the pickets was to pretend to be French, and between the three of them, they knew maybe ten words.

"It's impossible," Uncas said to his father in Algonquian. The old chief agreed, and the two raced over to hide behind a boulder with Hawkeye.

"There's no way through, Father."

"No, there isn't, Hawkeye."

"So what do we do, father?" Uncas questioned.

"We get some powder and lead, and go back to save the girls."

"But even if we save them from Magua, how will we get them through here?"

"Those ladies have one skill none of us have: they know French, and the major likely does too. If we can just get them to talk for us, we may all get in," Chingachgook explained.

Hawkeye grinned. "Brilliant as always, Father," He ran over to the body of the Wendat and retrieved the musket, powder horn, and ammunition.

"How much?"

"Not enough."

"Quickly, then. Let us away," Chingachgook urged.

The men kept their heads low but began running toward the pickets. The closer they got, the more Wendats and soldiers they would encounter.

Hawkeye gave a piercing whistle, and the three men all slid behind trees. Two Wendats were approaching them, speaking in Wyandot. Though Hawkeye couldn't understand the language, the tone was clearly casual; they were unaware of the Mohicans' presence.

Chingachgook and Uncas jumped out from behind the trees and ripped the muskets out of the men's hands, shoving them to the ground. They pounced on the men, pinning them and putting a hand over each of their mouths.

Hawkeye knelt beside their captives.

"Forgive us, but we need your weapons and supplies. We aren't going to hurt you, but we can't have you following us either. We are going to tie you up so you can't attack us, but we'll allow you to return to the pickets."

The Wendats were staring up at Hawkeye, wide-eyed. He knew he was an intimidating man, but it still always shocked him how easily he could scare other grown men.

He nodded toward his brother and father. "They are going to uncover your mouths, but before you think of screaming, let me introduce you to Killdeer." He brought his rifle in front of him, displaying it for the men. "This is Killdeer. It's fifty inches, one of the most accurate pieces on this continent. Before I had Killdeer, it belonged to Tom Hutter, a pirate. Hutter was scalped and left to die.[1] "

The Wendats gulped.

"If you make a noise, I will use Killdeer to kill you. You haven't got a hope of escape; I don't miss."

Uncas and Chingachgook removed their hands from the Wendats' mouths and began taking all the useful supplies from them, tossing them to Hawkeye. He examined their new inventory while his father and brother bound the men's hands behind their backs.

"Alright, let them go."

The Wendats went scampering away from the three men, not making a sound. Once they were out of sight, the Mohicans began laughing.

---

1. This is a reference to the actual way Hawkeye got Killdeer in The Leatherstocking Tales. However, in the original series, Hawkeye is much older than Uncas, around Chingachgook's age, and Uncas had not been born yet.

"That was deceitful, my son," said Chingachgook.

"I told no lies!"

"The Mingoes killed Thomas Hutter."

"I didn't say I did!"

Uncas patted his brother on the shoulder. "Killdeer isn't loaded, so how would you presume to kill them?"

"I didn't say I would shoot them! Perhaps I would bash them to death with it."

"You wouldn't risk hurting it like that."

"I could impale them with my ramrod for all you know!"

Chingachgook chuckled, shaking his head. "*La Longue Carabine* is too smart for his own good."

13
The Clearing

10:17

Magua entered the cave where Cora, Alice, and Heyward were sitting. David stood in the corner, reading his psalm book silently. They all turned to face him.

"To your feet."

No one moved. They just stared at him.

"Come in, get them up!" Magua yelled in Wyandot over his shoulder.

Three of his men rushed into the cave from outside and began yelling at them. One pointed his gun at the major and gestured for him to rise. The older sister jumped to her feet and pulled the younger one up with her. She stood between her and Magua's men.

The three men looked to Magua for instructions, and he nodded toward the major. Hatirontha grabbed Heyward's wrists and tied them together. He also wrapped rope around the man's upper arms, pinning them to his body.

Sayowahes led the group through the back exit of the cave, ducking through the small passageway that connected the sections. Once they reached the exit, they had to walk one by one behind the falls because the ledge was very thin.

The ledge was slippery, covered in moss moistened by the water of the falls. Magua trailed behind the dark-haired sister. She had one hand on the edge of the wall, the other grasping her dress and lifting it as she stepped gingerly along the ledge. She was wearing riding boots, which were not exactly made for traversing this terrain.

Her shoe found a slick spot and she lost her balance. She screamed as her arms swung wildly, grasping for something to gain purchase on. Magua slipped his hand around her waist and pulled her back onto the ledge.

"Careful, miss, you wouldn't want to fall to your Yengee death," he said, smirking at her. Cora glared at him and walked closer to the wall than before. The group reached the other side, and the men began corralling them into the canoes that waited at the edge of the river.

They paddled off down the river. The ladies remained quiet, the dark-haired sister held her sister's hand, and ran her hand over her hair. The singer played a soft melody on his flute. It seemed to calm the sisters, but Magua rolled his eyes at the display.

Magua sat behind Major Heyward and discussed everything with Sayowahes in Wyandot.

"Where are we going now, my brother?" Sayowahes questioned.

"To the village north of Caniaderi Guarunte.[1]"

"And have you decided what you are going to do with them there?"

"I have," Magua answered, not explaining further.

"You are not going to tell me?"

"Of course not!"

---

1. Lake Champlain was called Caniaderi Guarunte by the Mohawks, and the name was used by several other tribes of the area, including the Wendats.

Sayowahes groaned.

"We are like brothers, Magua, can you not share everything with me?"

"There are some things I must keep to myself."

"Very well, but maybe next time I have information to share, I will be just as reluctant to tell you!"

Magua laughed.

The canoe came to a stop at the edge of the river, where it was calm and not as fast-flowing as it had been earlier. The men jumped out of the canoes and pulled the ladies out as well. Sayowahes grabbed Alice by the wrist. The girl cringed as he pushed her wrists together and tied them. Hatirontha then did the same to Cora. Major Heyward was given the same treatment, although the rope was wound around his arms, keeping them locked against his torso. David was left untied.

The group was led through the woods, the ladies being dragged by their captors. A stray branch caught Cora's sleeve, ripping it. She muttered something under her breath. Magua eyed the woman, curious if she would say something to him. She said nothing, but wore a scowl.

Suddenly, Alice's foot caught the bottom of her skirt, and the poor girl tumbled to her knees, Sayowahes only keeping her upright by holding the rope. The ladies' skirts were made for riding horses, not tramping through the forest.

"Stop!" Magua commanded. All of his men halted instantly and Magua turned around, walking back toward the ladies. He looked down at their skirts and pulled out a knife, handing it to them.

"What does he want us to do, Cora?" Alice asked.

"The skirts, they are slowing you down," Magua answered for her. "Cut them, or I will." He once again offered Cora the knife. Cora nodded and began cutting down the length and layers of her skirt. Then she turned and gave her sister's frock the same treatment.

Magua, seeing that this was done, held out his hand and gestured for her to give the knife back. For a second or two, Cora's grip tightened on the knife, staring up at Magua with fire behind her eyes. Magua could tell that she was debating whether it was worth it to try and fight him here.

"Cora... Please." Alice said. "Cora, he has us. Even if you kill one, there are five more to take his place."

Magua smirked. "Your fair sister is correct," he said, grabbing her wrist, spinning her to face her sister, and pinning her arm behind her back. He held her against his chest and chuckled in her ear.

"If you want to survive, I would take your sister's advice. As entertaining as your fire is, I must snuff it out, at least for now..." he uttered the last sentence, trailing off. He pushed Cora away from him, taking the knife out of her hand as he did so.

The group continued their march for another two hours. They finally came to a clearing.

"Rest, you'll need it." Magua sent a few men off to find food and instructed another of them to build a fire. He watched the ladies and the major sit beside a tree as the psalmodist knelt off to the side, his head dipped in prayer.

If only they knew.

14
Magua's Offer
15:03

The group sat in a circle, passing around the water skin that Magua had given them. Cora had an arm wrapped around her sister, as Alice was becoming panicked and anxious. Cora's gaze flashed to where Magua sat. He was obviously deep in thought, staring at the ground with a face carved with intensity. A few of Magua's men were standing a few yards away, watching the group and speaking to each other in Wyandot.

"Will they keep moving us, Cora?" Alice asked, squeezing her sister's hand.

"I'm not sure, flower." Cora stole further glances at Magua.

Heyward had tried to manipulate Magua, but Cora did not think the Wendat chief could be fooled so easily. He was clever: a real fox.

"Major Heyward, come here! Now!" Magua suddenly shouted.

The major's head shot up. He pushed himself to his feet as best he could with his hands bound. He walked over toward Magua, who had situated himself on a rock behind a group of bushes.

"Go to the elder sister, tell her I mean to speak with her," Magua said.

"You wish to speak to Miss Munro?"

"The father will listen to what the daughter says, not the officer," Magua replied.

"Ah, I see." Heyward turned and returned to Alice and Cora.

"What did he say?" Cora asked.

"It seems as if he is interested in my deal. He just wants to have your word, Miss Munro. He does not take mine for truth."

Heyward's chin was lifted, and a small smile played on his lips.

"My word?" Cora asked.

"Yes, you're the colonel's daughter, so in Magua's eyes, you would have more sway over the colonel than a mere major," Heyward explained.

Cora nodded. "I understand."

"David, watch over Alice," Cora said, nodding toward her younger sister.

The psalmodist scooted closer to Alice and held out his flute, offering it for her to try.

Heyward helped Cora to her feet.

Cora cast a glance over her shoulder at her sister, who was blowing lightly on the flute. Cora hesitated before stepping with Heyward toward Magua.

"When the Huron talks to the women, the tribes shut their ears," Magua said, upon seeing that Heyward had accompanied the daughter of Munro to their meeting. At first Heyward did not move, eyes flitting to Cora, a frown on his face.

Cora nodded toward her sister. "Please go to Alice, Major, and comfort her with our remaining prospects."

Heyward nodded. "As you wish, Miss Munro."

Cora forced a smile and followed Magua as he led her behind the bushes to where he had been sitting.

"What would *Le Renard* say to the daughter of Colonel Munro?"

Magua's face was unreadable.

"Listen," he began, taking a step toward the woman. "Magua was born a chief and a warrior among the Wendats of the lakes. He saw the suns of fifteen summers make the snows of fifteen winters run off in the streams before he saw a white man; and until he saw a white man in the woods, he was happy." He stared briefly off into the trees behind her.

"Then Magua met some young men in the woods, men who taught him to drink liquor. They were good friends with bad morals. This is where I learned French and English. We became lethargic and lazy, and we drank our days away. Magua enjoyed his time with Antoine and Robert, but soon enough he fell into the hands of the Yengees."

"Yengees?" Cora probed.

"They who fought the white men of the Canadas," Magua clarified.

"I see."

"I was accepted by the Mohawks who fought for the Yengees. The Yengees took the Mohawks and made them fight the Wendats. And when I took up the knife against my people, a white chief led the way. My white chief, the old chief at the lake, your father, led his warriors against my people, the Hurons. Magua obeyed the orders and slew his brothers, until he came to the village of his family.

"However, when Munro ordered the destruction of the village, I stood in the way. My father, my mother, my two sisters lay in that village. All as innocent as the daisies in the wood. Munro demanded I stand aside, and I did not. So, he sent his men into the village, and they found them, my family." Magua's voice was almost breaking as he told the story, his eyes boring into Cora's face. "What did Munro do? Let his daughter say!"

"He forgot not his words, and did justice by punishing the offender," she said.

"Justice! Justice? Is it justice to make evil, and then punish for it?"
Cora didn't answer, only staring into his eyes.

"They were brought before me, all of them. He threw my sisters to his men, who had their way with them, and then he killed them all. When this was done, and the village had been burned, I was dragged back to the fort and caged. I sat in the dark for three days before your father dragged me out before the white men and tied me to the stake." Magua's voice had regained its strength and it rose with each sentence he uttered. "The Wendat chief was whipped like a dog!" Magua shouted, ripping open his vest that set him apart from his countrymen.

"See!" There were scars along his chest, thin and white from the cuts of so many blades. Even a bullet wound decorated his chest. "Here are the scars of knives and bullets-of these a warrior may boast before his nation, but the white chief has left scars on the back of the Wendat chief[1] that he must hide like a woman," Magua explained, turning and pulling his hair aside, that Cora might look upon the scars that decorated his back. True to his word, long, raised, white scars ran back and forth across his back, covering every inch of it.

"I had thought that an Indian warrior was patient, that his spirit felt not, and knew not the pain his body suffered," the undaunted girl replied, her lip set in a firm line and her fists balled at her side.

---

1. In this adaptation it is canon that Magua is very good with languages, and would not be apt to refer to himself in the third person. In Cooper's book he often spoke this way to suggest a lack of understanding of the language. There are certain parts in this adaptation where I have kept this verbiage because it is more dramatic (and Magua is an incredibly dramatic individual).

"When the Chippewas tied Magua to the stake and cut this gash, the Wendat laughed in their faces and told them, 'Women struck so light!' His spirit was then in the clouds! But when he felt the blows of Munro, his spirit lay under the birch. The spirit of a Wendat remembers forever!"

"And yet it may be appeased. If my father has done you this injustice, show him how a Huron chief can forgive an injury, and take back his daughters. You have heard from Major Heyward—"

"Never!" Magua cut her off.

"What then would you have?" she demanded.

"What a Huron loves—good for good; bad for bad!"

"You would then revenge the injury and suffering inflicted by Munro on his innocent daughters? Would it not be more like a man to go before his face, and take the satisfaction of a warrior?"

"The arms of the white men are long, and their knives sharp! Why should *Le Renard* go among the muskets of his warriors, when he holds the spirit of Munro in his hand?"

"For God's sake, Magua, tell us your intentions! Tell us why you have taken us and what you mean to do," Cora demanded. "Is there no way of releasing the anger in your heart without harming us, his helpless daughters?" She paused, biting back tears. "At least, release my innocent sister. Let her go and pour out all your malice on me. Purchase wealth with her safety and satisfy your revenge with a single victim. I will gladly die to see her safely returned to our father!" Tears poured down her cheeks. "Losing both of his daughters would send my father to the grave, and how may you harm him there?"

Magua stared at her for a second, then nodded.

"Listen, woman. Let the light-haired daughter of the Yengees' chief go to her father at the lake and tell her father what has been done, as long as the dark-haired daughter will swear to tell no lie," he said, taking a step toward her again.

Cora retreated a step.

"What must I promise?" she asked in a quiet voice.

She clenched her jaw, forcing herself to remain civil.

"When Magua was stolen from his tribe, his woman was given to another chief; he has now made friends with the Wendats and will return to the graves of his fathers on the shore of the great lake. Let the daughter of Munro follow him and live in his longhouse as his woman."

Cora's face remained impassive, though her heart was now racing. *For what reason could Magua possibly offer this option?*

The blood rushed to her head, but she kept her composure, and with the gentility of her sex, replied to the man.

"And what pleasure would Magua find in sharing his home with a woman he did not love? It would be better to take the gold of Munro and buy the heart of a Huron woman with his gifts," she replied, her eyes refusing to leave his own. *Le Renard* didn't respond for a minute, seemingly processing her answer.

"Is this the response of a woman disgusted by me, or a daughter determined to return to her father?" His voice was on edge. Clearly, her response would dictate her and her comrades' fates, so she bit her tongue, keeping back the retort she wished to give.

"Magua, I am not disgusted by you as much as I simply do not love you. I do not wish to marry without love. I wish to return to my father, but if I must die or...follow you to allow my sister to keep her life, I am willing."

He nodded, accepting this answer. "You must know your future, smart woman. You would draw my water, you would hoe my corn, and cook my venison. The body of Munro would sleep among the

cannon, but his heart would lie within reach of *Le Renard*'s knife,"
Magua said, reaching out his hand to gain purchase on her arm. She
wrenched her arm free, pulling away from the offender.

"Monster! Well you deserve your treacherous name!" Cora cried
out, her eyes burning with hate. "None but a fiend could meditate
such vengeance! But you overrate your power! You shall find it is in
truth the heart of Munro you hold, and that will defy your utmost
malice!" She turned away from the offender and stalked back to her
companions.

Magua was shouting to his tribesmen, ordering them to collect the
prisoners.

"Go! Read your fortunes in his face!" Cora said to her comrades,
who looked on in confusion at the rallying of the Wendats. Heyward
demanded to know what had occurred, but Cora was too disturbed
to explain the situation to him.

Cora grabbed her sister's hand. "I love you," she said.

Magua's men rushed them. When Heyward stepped between them
and the ladies, the Wendats viciously attacked him, knocking him to
the ground and kicking him.

"No, stop!" Alice screamed, crying.

One of the men grabbed Alice by the wrist and pulled her away
from Cora.

"Please, oh God, please don't hurt her!" Cora begged, falling to her
knees.

The warrior dragged Alice to one of the thin trees that lined the
clearing. She didn't fight as he pressed her against it, tying her wrists
together behind it. A steady stream of tears fell down her face.

The men who had been beating Heyward pulled him up to his feet
and shoved him against another tree, tying him there.

Cora stared up at Magua, who advanced on her, his face flat and emotionless.

"Magua, please," she murmured as he reached her.

He gave no response, instead grabbing her arm and yanking her to her feet. He led her over to the tree between Alice and Heyward and pressed her against it, nodding at one of his men to bind her wrists while he studied her face.

David now stood off to the side, watching the group while playing a calm hymn on his flute.

Magua watched Cora, gripping his knife tightly in his hand. His expression was cold, and his eyes were red-rimmed.

"What says Cora?" Magua demanded. "Is her head too good to find a pillow in the home of Magua? Will she like it better if it rolls about the hillside, a plaything for wolves?" he taunted, holding his knife up to her face.

Alice's face turned white. "What does he mean, Cora?"

"Nothing, flower. He means nothing at all. He is a barbarous and ignorant man, hell-bent on vengeance and nothing else." Cora delivered her response with dignity and disgust. Magua had been wronged by her father, but what fair and rational man would respond by demanding the man's daughter as his wife or else kill her and her sister? The demand Magua had made was inconceivable. "Let us use our dying breaths to ask our Father's forgiveness and pardon."

"Pardon?" Magua echoed, his voice rising in anger. "The arms of the Huron are longer than the Yengees, their mercy shorter," he started. Now the man turned to the light-haired daughter, cocking his head to the side. "Speak, shall I send the younger daughter to her father, and will you follow me into the woods?"

"Leave me be," Cora begged. "You mingle bitterness in my prayers. You stand between us and our God."

Magua took a step back from the elder Munro daughter and moved toward her fairer sister. He unsheathed his knife, holding it to the young girl's face.

"Look!" he taunted. "The child weeps; she is too young to die! Will you not send her back to her father, to a life of safety and love? Must you be the cause of such a pure creature's death?"

Alice looked over at her sister, her brows pressed together, her mouth slightly parted.

"Cora, what does the man mean? Has he spoken of returning me to Father?" Alice asked, her head turned so that she might look upon her sister's rigid form.

"He offers us all life, my sister. Not just you and me, but Duncan and David as well. And that he would send the three of you to our father, if only..." Cora paused, choking on the words before she could utter them.

"If only what, dear sister? Oh, that he would send us to Papa! Whatever he has requested, it must be worth the sacrifice!"

"To buy this freedom, I would have to follow him, to stay with him as a life partner, in the woods until the day I die. So, speak now, my flower. What would you have me do? For you, I would lay down my life, and for you, I would ruin myself," Cora said, turning to look upon the now-quaking figure of her sister.

"Oh, such a proposal! Surely you jest with our misery, dear sister! I could never ask something like this of you, you must know?" Alice replied, tears falling from her eyes.

"Such I knew would be your answer!" replied Cora. She turned to Magua, who was watching on, his eyes dark and hard. "Magua, so you have heard, we are to leave this life as we have lived it—together."

"Then die!" Magua shouted, hurling his hatchet at Alice. Somehow, the girl's head swerved to the side, and the axe became lodged in the tree, severing off one of her blonde curls. She strained against the rope that bound her, trying to wrench herself free from certain death.

"Tsawenhohi.[2]" Magua nodded toward the girl, and the man he had addressed took out his own hatchet and prepared to throw it as well.

Heyward strained at the rope binding him to a nearby sapling.

The man wound up to throw his hatchet, but before he could release it he was thrown to the ground by Heyward, who, having been released by the slick psalmodist, tackled the Wendat to the ground. The Wendats around them held up their rifles, but Magua stopped them, not wanting Tsawenhohi to be shot.

But before Tsawenhohi could release it, Heyward, having been released by the slick psalmodist, tackled the Wendat to the ground. All the Wendats around them raised their rifles, but Magua shook his head.

Before Tsawenhohi could release his hatchet Heyward tore away from the tree, tearing the ropes that bound him in two. Heyward tackled Tsawenhohi and the two rolled around on the forest floor, trying to get the upper hand. All the Wendats around them raised their rifles, but Magua shook his head and raised a hand to stop them

David, who had loosened Heyward's binds, began playing his flute as loud as he could and dancing around the ladies. The Wendats glanced at him, but were too busy watching the fight to pay him much mind.

The men struggled against each other, each trying to overcome the other before Tsawenhohi gained the upper hand. He shoved Heyward to the ground, raising his hatchet to strike him.

---

2. The name Tsawenhohi means "Vulture" in Wyandot.

BANG!

Tsawenhohi fell back away from Heyward, clutching his abdomen where blood poured out. The air cleared, and the figure of Hawkeye, his rifle still raised, materialized amidst the dissipating smoke.

The Wendats all panicked, trying to ready their arms again. But they were too slow. The Mohicans and Hawkeye entered the clearing, and the Mohicans shot two more of the Wendats. Hawkeye threw himself into the fight, cutting through any other Wendats foolish enough to engage him.

Uncas tackled another of the Wendats, knocking the man to the ground and thrusting his knife into the warrior's chest. The man cried out and blood seeped from the edges of his mouth.

From the side, Magua watched the events, slowly backing away from the violence. Eventually, he called away the remaining Wendats, who followed him, sprinting into the woods. Chingachgook wound up and threw his hatchet, the blade catching one of them in the back as they fled.

The men rushed to the ladies. Heyward practically shoved Hawkeye out of the way, so that he might be the one to untie the fair maiden. Uncas sliced the ropes that bound the eldest Miss Munro's hands and gently held up her wrist to examine the rope marks that had been left there.

"Are you hurt?" he asked, looking down at her. She held eye contact while shaking her head.

"I am well, thank you. You've saved us once again," she said, smiling up at him.

"I told you I would return, did I not?" he asked, now holding both of her hands in his own.

"You did, but I thought Magua might kill us before you ever had the chance to reach us." Cora threw her arms around the man. "Oh,

Uncas, his plans were terrible." She turned to look at the tree where the hatchet was still embedded.

"What do you mean, Cora?"

"Magua asked me to go with him, Uncas. He wanted me to take the place of the woman he had lost when he began serving my father. He even offered as much as letting the others go, if I only followed him into the woods," Cora explained.

Uncas' face contorted. He pulled Cora tighter and wrapped his arms around her body. She was stiff at first, but quickly melted into his embrace.

"I am truly sorry that he tried such a thing. And to threaten the life of your sister, horrid. I will protect you from him!" Uncas declared. Cora smiled to herself, her head against his chest.

"We must move, Magua will surely attack us tomorrow. We need to be close enough to the fort that he wouldn't dare," Chingachgook said, motioning northwest with his head.

"Where will we go tonight, *Le Gros Serpent*?" Heyward asked.

"Somewhere Magua wouldn't dare follow us." Chingachgook looked at his sons, and they both nodded. The men silently led the group away from the clearing toward the west. The ladies met each other's eyes, pursing their lips, but said nothing.

Heyward patted David on the back, thanking him for his timely assistance.

15
The Cemetery
19:57

By the time the group reached their destination, night had fallen. They walked into what appeared to be a clearing. There was a shack of sorts, with just three walls and a ceiling. It looked abandoned, and the grass in the clearing was long. It seemed as though no one had walked there in years, perhaps even decades.

Cora noted that Uncas placed his feet with care, and his eyes darted around. He approached the edge of the clearing and then stopped, his face pale, as he looked at the grassy area ahead of them.

Chingachgook walked into the grass with Hawkeye, and the two both turned back to look at Uncas. He looked quickly between them and the ground they tread on. His father motioned for him to follow, and he obliged, taking small steps into the grass to join his family. Cora watched on in confusion.

"Why are you afraid?" she asked as she got closer to the three men.

"This is a burial ground," Uncas responded. He nodded toward the ground and it occurred to Cora for the first time that small ridges dotted the clearing. People had been buried there, and judging by the state of the building and the length of the grass, it was some time ago.

"A graveyard?" she asked.

"Yes, ma'am, a graveyard," Hawkeye answered. "The men that lie there are both friend and foe. They attacked our village, and with them died the last of my family's tribe."

"The village was here?" Cora asked.

"No ma'am, the village was west of here. We tracked the Wendats down after they attacked, but most of us didn't make it," Hawkeye answered.

"You all fought here?" Alice asked.

"Yes, Miss Alice," Uncas said. "We are the only ones to survive the fight, from either side."

"And why are you afraid?" Cora asked.

"The men, if they were not scalped, they would haunt us for treading upon their graves. We checked everyone, but what if we missed one? I cannot be sure…" Uncas trailed off.

"Scalping?" Cora questioned.

"We believe scalping releases the man's… What's the word?" Hawkeye started, before turning to his brother for assistance.

"Soul."

"Right, yes, well if you leave a man unscalped, you keep him from going to the hunting grounds of the afterlife. He hates you for it, and if you walk on his grave without releasing him of his burden, he treats you as guilty too."

"So the… scalping… It is done for religious reasons, not for trophies?" Cora asked.

"Generally speaking, but all men who take scalps have their own reasons," Hawkeye said. "Many British soldiers take them too. I would think those are for trophies, or maybe just some sort of sick mockery."

"British soldiers take scalps?" Alice questioned, her voice rising in surprise. She turned toward Heyward.

"Is this true, Major?"

"Indeed, ma'am, mostly enlisted men, the infantrymen. They are usually very disturbed men; they have seen things that most others haven't. This can... ruin a man."

"How barbaric... I know they must be under horrible pressures and stress, but to take war trophies such as those... That is truly savage," Alice said.

Heyward nodded.

"Right, well, this has been a lovely conversation, but I rather think you ladies ought to get to sleep," Hawkeye said, gesturing toward the shelter.

Cora nodded and led her sister inside, taking a seat against the wall.

"I will take first watch," Heyward said.

"No, no, Major. You will sleep," Chingachgook urged.

"But I must help. I must defend these ladies. It is my responsibility!" Heyward argued.

"Major Heyward, if we lie within the tents of the 60th, I could not ask for a better watchman, but—" Hawkeye started.

"Thank you, sir," Heyward cut him off.

Hawkeye's brow rose.

"*But* in the forest you are blind and you are dumb as a child, so *please* take your rest and be prepared in the morning for our long hike," he urged.

Duncan scowled, but said nothing as he moved over to settle against the outside of the wall that the ladies were lying against.

The two Mohicans went out in different directions to guard, circling the area slowly so that they could see any foe that might attempt to approach them. Hawkeye sat in the middle, on a stump, overseeing the entire area.

David approached Hawkeye and requested to sit next to the scout. Hawkeye nodded and watched the silly man take a seat beside him. Hawkeye was surprised he had made it this far. It was true that the Wendats didn't usually kill those they viewed as mad, but David had meddled. He had untied Heyward and surely done other things as well. Hawkeye refused to believe Magua would allow him to live if he knew how he had helped them.

"How are you holding up?" Hawkeye asked the man, tapping his head to indicate David's wound.

"Very well, thank you for asking, sir. I know it must not seem it, but this is not my first time running through the woods and being in contact with Indians."

"Really? I never would have guessed," Hawkeye admitted. "Where were you before you came here?"

"Down in Virginia, I was a preacher there. I had to leave when the locals found out my real work."

"Oh?"

David leaned in close to Hawkeye. "Do not let the major know, but I was in the slave-freeing business."

"Why should the major not know?" Hawkeye questioned, already having an idea of the answer.

"He's from the south, and an officer, which means he's rich. You know how people get rich in the South?"

"Ah, I see. Well, that is very brave work, David. How did they discover you?"

"One of the little boys I had hidden in my basement got panicky because I hadn't been able to get his mother out yet, and he ran back to find her. The little boy's sister told me where he went, and I arranged an emergency escape for me and those who were hiding with me."

"How many have you saved?"

"Oh, I'm not sure. I used to be a Quaker, you know. We did a lot of work like that, but when I left the church, I did it all by myself," he said.

"A Quaker?" Hawkeye asked, slightly amused by that.

"Why yes, sir. I was a Quaker until I realized I had a fundamental disagreement with them; I believe that violence is often necessary to protect the innocent."

Hawkeye smiled down at the man at his feet. Clearly, David was a good man and much smarter than any of them had given him credit for. He told the man as much, and David nodded, thanking him.

"All the glory be to God," he said, lowering his eyes and placing his palms together. Hawkeye smiled at that too. He might not have understood the religion of these people, but if they were all as devoted to their God and spreading his love, the world would certainly be a better place.

The scout sat there for an hour or so before he made out the figure of his father racing toward him. He jumped to his feet, raising an eyebrow at his father.

"Hurons!" Chingachgook hissed.

Hawkeye's eyes bugged and he nodded toward Uncas. Chingachgook raced off to get his son, and Hawkeye walked over to the hut, David following him. He woke Heyward and nodded toward the inside of the hut.

Crawling around the corner, Heyward huddled behind the wall. The Mohicans ran up and joined the rest of the group. All the men raised their guns, ready to fire, as they all hid behind the wall. The ladies awoke, their eyes full of fear as they watched the men prepare to fight.

Hawkeye heard the padding feet of approaching Wendats. He put his head against the wall and peeked through a tiny crack in the planks. He held a hand up to let the other men know they hadn't been spotted yet, and he kept it there as he watched the encroaching force intently.

There were perhaps twenty of them, all carrying the cheap muskets that the French gave their infantrymen and native allies. They crept in the direction of the hut. The group all held their breath. If the Wendats entered the clearing and stepped onto the grass, it would mean they didn't know the significance of the field, and, without any cover, the group would have nowhere to hide. But if the natives entered the clearing and backed off, the group would be safe.

The Wendat in the front took a step forward, his foot inches from the grass, and he looked around, eyeing the hut and then the mounds of dirt with overgrown grass. Everyone in the group held their breath, watching his next move. His eyes widened, and he took a step back, muttering something to his comrades. They all backed up, trying to get away as quickly as possible.

Hawkeye and Uncas grinned at each other.

It had worked.

"Well, Alice, I suppose you can tell your father that you were saved by Mohicans and Hurons alike; some of them were just long dead," Hawkeye whispered, chuckling.

"*Miss* Alice," Heyward said, correcting the scout.

"I apologize if I've offended your *delicate nature*, Major, but the lady told me to call her by her given name, no title, so you may answer to her," Hawkeye said, testing.

"I... That is her p-prerogative, I suppose," the man stuttered.

"Yes, it is," Hawkeye returned, keeping his voice level and non-threatening. Heyward didn't respond. Alice looked up at Hawkeye, biting her lip.

"We have a few more hours before it's light enough to travel again; we'll need the light to traverse down the hillside to the fort, and we'll need our wits about us to make it through the French pickets," Chingachgook said.

The ladies nodded, and Cora lay back against the wall, her sister's head in her lap. She ran her fingers through Alice's hair.

Hawkeye turned to go back to the lookout stump, but stole a glance at Alice, smiling to himself.

5 August 1757

16
Fort William Henry

09:34

T he group reached the top of the hill and looked down on the scene before them. It was hard to see much of anything through the fog and smoke, but the ladies could just make out the shape of the fort. Sure enough, the British flag still flew, but cannons were firing every few seconds, and smoke enveloped the fort.

"There it is, ladies," Hawkeye said, motioning toward the fort on the lake. It was somewhat shaped like a square, with watch towers on each corner that jutted out from the rest of the walls. "You've traveled thousands of miles to be here, and now you are just hours from seeing your father," he proclaimed.

"Hours?" Alice questioned. "It doesn't seem so far away."

"It may not look so far, dear lady, but between us and that fort is an army. A French army that will not take kindly to a group trying to sneak into the fort they are trying to besiege. Your father has been unable to receive any couriers throughout the siege, so getting you to him will take time and care," the hunter explained.

"I hope that I can be of assistance," Heyward said. "I can distract or confuse our enemy with my French. As long as they cannot see me, I will be safe."

"We are actually counting on them seeing you," Hawkeye said.

Heyward raised an eyebrow. "What do you mean? My uniform would give me away."

"Maybe, but these uniforms will not," Hawkeye said, pushing aside the bush next to them to reveal five French infantrymen's uniforms.

"Are you ladies up to the task?" Hawkeye questioned.

The sisters gave each other a sideways glance, but nodded. "Very well, we will give you ladies your privacy as you get dressed into those uniforms, and should you have any questions, I am sure that the major knows how they are to be worn." Hawkeye turned to the psalmodist. "You too, David," he said.

David nodded, picking up the pile of clothes and following the other men away so the ladies could change in private. The ladies began undressing each other, pulling off their garments. The original owners of the uniforms had clearly been young and thin because the uniforms were almost a perfect fit. Cora and Alice pulled their hair back into ponytails and then looked each other up and down to ensure they did not appear female in any way.

"Can you imagine us in powdered wigs?" Alice joked. Cora chortled, then the two called out that they were decent. The men came around the corner. The sisters were amused to see David wearing the getup, his hair pulled back like theirs, his large knees straining in the trousers.

"Very well, let us go," Chingachgook said. The group descended the hill, getting closer and closer to the pickets of the French. Cora and Alice both had muskets over their shoulders while the Mohicans only carried their knives and hatchets.

The group finally reached the pickets and they began conversing in French to blend in. Nobody paid them any attention until they got to the front of the pickets. A man approached the group, and the ladies tensed.

"Who sent you to join me?" he asked in French.

"The very king himself!" Heyward said, giving a convincing fake laugh. The man chuckled and patted him on the back.

"Very well. Who are the Indians?"

"Some animals that were sent with me. I wasn't told why," Heyward responded, shrugging his shoulders.

Alice cringed.

The man laughed again and nodded, welcoming them to his post.

The group stood guard there for around five hours, occasionally conversing in French about mundane topics to keep their cover secure. The night began to fall and with it came the next stage in their plan.

"You can sleep first. I'll keep watch," Cora offered in a suitably gruff voice. The man nodded and lay down against the stump he had been sitting on. The second he began snoring, the Mohicans sprang on him.

They swiftly gagged him and bound his hands behind his back. His eyes were big and pleading, his body shaking with whimpers. Uncas dragged him under a bush to hide him from his comrades, and they bound his legs as well.

"Awfully sorry, friend, but we have to get into that fort," Heyward said to the man in French as they pushed the brush over him. Then they began creeping toward the fort, their hands raised above their heads. The men on the parapet had their guns trained on them as they got closer.

"Take another step closer and you're dead men!" one of the lookouts shouted.

Chingachgook motioned for them to stop, and the group halted.

Alice and Cora ripped off their caps and pulled their hair out of their ponytails. The men above them gaped in shock.

"We are Cora and Alice Munro. Let us in so that we may see our father!" Cora called out.

The lookouts stared for a second, then nodded, calling down to the men at the gate.

"You must go now, ladies, and be safe with your father," Chingachgook said in a solemn voice.

The girls turned to him.

"You are not coming with us?" Alice asked, tears already forming in her eyes.

"No, Chulëntët. My sons and I do not belong here; we were made to live on the move, not stuck in a fort," he said, putting a hand on her shoulder.

"Oh Chingachgook!" she said, throwing her arms around the aging Mohican. "I am going to miss you so much, but we will see each other again! I demand it!"

Chingachgook patted Alice's back and kissed her forehead.

"Someday, my dear, we will."

Alice turned to Hawkeye and Uncas, hugging both of them as well. The men held her gently between them, and Hawkeye mussed up her hair a bit.

"Stay safe, Alice," Hawkeye said.

She looked up at him.

"And you as well, Hawkeye."

Cora said goodbye to Chingachgook and Hawkeye before turning to Uncas. He smiled at her, but his gaze was downcast.

"Fear not, my lady, I will see you again," he promised her. She blushed, smiling at the man.

"Yes, yes you will," she said. He plucked her hand from her side and brought it up to meet his lips. He placed a gentle kiss there before dropping her hand and urging her toward the door that was now opening.

The ladies nodded, turning to run into the fort, then glancing back one more time at the men they were leaving behind them.

"Cora! Alice!" the old colonel shouted upon seeing his daughters. The girls ran up to their father, almost knocking him to the ground with their hugs.

"Father!" they both shouted, showering him with hugs and kisses.

"Why on earth would you continue on when you learned we were under siege?" he demanded, turning to Major Heyward.

"Sir, I..." the major started.

"Father, it was I who insisted we continue to the fort!" Cora interrupted, saving Major Heyward a verbal lashing. "Alice and I were frightened that something would happen to you during the siege. How could we not come?"

"Very well, I canna be upset with ya for that!" Munro said. "To be honest, I canna be upset with ya at all. Oh, my dear daughters, how I have missed ya so!"

"Oh, Papa, we are here now! We are with you, and we will stay with you until you are relieved of your duty," Alice said, resting her head on her aging father's shoulder.

Munro smiled. "It is so good to have you back," he said, pulling them both into a hug.

"Now, I believe you will be needing a bath, and certainly a change of clothes! And once you are clean and clothed, you can tell me everything!" the man said. He shooed his girls off to follow the sergeant, who would lead them to the washroom.

17
The Argument

12:00

Colonel Munro's head rose at the knock on his door. He watched his eldest daughter walk in. She had bathed and was clothed in a clean, forest green dress. Upon seeing her like this, he realized his daughter was all grown up. She was twenty years old, and he had been gone for over half her life.

"Ah, Cora, my dear, come in !" he called.

Cora obliged, walking over to him. She stood in front of his desk and glowered down at him.

"We need to talk," she said.

Munro could detect the anger in her tone, but he could not think of what he could have done to already upset her.

"Of course, my dear. What would you have us talk about?"

"Magua," she replied in a clipped tone.

Munro's eyebrows scrunched together when she pronounced the Wendat's name.

"Magua? I know that name, where do I know it from?" he thought aloud.

"Oh, where indeed?!" Cora said through gritted teeth. "He is a Huron, a man who was under your control. You killed his family, Papa!

You let your men...violate his sisters, and then, after all of that, you whipped him!"

"Oh, Magua. Yes, I remember him."

"Papa, how could you be so calm? Your actions were inhuman!" Cora shouted at her father.

"Inhuman? They are inhuman! This Magua is inhuman; he is a savage!" The colonel was now on his feet. He had certainly not expected to be yelled at by his daughter, especially not about this.

"Savage?" Cora shouted. "Savage like my mother?" She took a step forward, yelling in his face.

"This has nothing to do with Magua's race! Your mother was a lady, the daughter of a gentleman! I would not have allowed what was done to Magua to happen if he was genteel, but he is a heathen, unloved by our God!"

"'But I say unto you, Love your enemies, bless them that curse you, do good to them that hate you... for if ye love them which love you, what reward have ye'?" the girl continued. "Matthew 5:44 and 46! Our God would have you love all, even the heathens!"

Munro's face screwed up in frustration. "What would you have me do? Have the man dragged before me so that I might beg his forgiveness? He will not have it, I am sure!"

"No, Father, it is too late for that." Cora's voice was calm now. "His heart has grown cold, frozen over, with no hope of ever thawing. And he has..." Cora grimaced. "...he has decided he will take his malice out on me," she finished.

"What can you possibly mean by this? What has that devil done?" Munro demanded, grabbing his daughter by her arm and shaking her. He did not regret what he had done to Magua, nor to any of the others in his village, but if the consequences included his offspring being harmed he could not bear it.

"Did Major Heyward not explain why it took so long for us to reach the fort?"

"He just told me you got caught in skirmishes with Hurons, which is what I had already assumed, given Montcalm's siege."

Cora sighed. "Magua was to be our guide to the fort. However, on the way, a scout intercepted us, sensing something was off, and he was right; Magua was leading us astray. With the help of the scout and his Mohican family, we escaped Magua's grasp and sought refuge in a cave to wait out the night. In the morning, Magua and his men attacked us once again. We ran out of ammunition and I convinced the men to leave us behind, to save themselves," she explained.

"They abandoned you?" Munro shouted, sitting down hard in his seat. "H-How dare they! I will have those men found and hanged!"

"I told them to, Papa. They would have died if they had stayed, and then there would have been no one to save us from the Hurons and Magua. Magua took us north. When we were resting, he spoke with me in private, told me his story, and agreed to release Alice, Major Heyward, and David if I agreed to follow him into the woods and marry him. I refused, and he tried to kill Alice in retaliation, Papa! This is when the scout and his Mohican family saved us. Because of what you did to Magua, he was intent on keeping me, and using me to take his revenge. To make you live your life knowing I would spend the rest of my days as his wife, nay as his slave. Had the Mohicans and Hawkeye not rescued us when they did, we might have all met a bloody end!"

"So, you are blaming me for that demon's evil plan?"

"Papa, how can you call him a demon? I do not condone Magua's actions, but only because it is us he hurt. If he had done as much to you, you would have deserved it!"

"Deserved? So you *are* taking his side!"

"I have and will always stand for what is right! You destroying his family and then punishing him for opposing it wasn't right!" she argued.

"Cora Munro, I will not have your blatant disrespect! I am your father!" he thundered at her.

"Give me a reason to respect you! I respect gentlemen, and as far as I am concerned, you are far from it!"

"Indeed?" Munro said, his knuckles whitening as he gripped the arms of his chair. "I could have killed Magua after his display of filial piety, but I allowed him to live. Was this not mercy?"

"Mercy, oh mercy indeed!" Cora spat. She spun on her heel, heading toward the door. "I do not wish to speak to you until you have realized your faults!" She slammed the door so hard behind her that it rattled on its hinges.

7 August 1757

18
Visiting the Infirmary

14:48

The infirmary stank of blood and death, but the Munro sisters remained composed. The lead surgeon had been hesitant to allow them in there in the first place. It was, after all, no place for ladies. It took the colonel himself speaking with the surgeon to convince him that his daughters, though certainly ladies, had seen enough blood and carnage to stomach visiting the wounded there.

There were cots lining the room. Too many to truly fit in there, but the fort was under siege. What else were they to do? Most of the men were missing limbs, or in some cases, half their faces. They spent all day moaning and crying in agony until sleep finally found them again.

Cora walked straight to the nearest man when she entered. He was missing half of his right leg and had a bandage wrapped around his head, almost covering his eyes. Compared to the others, he was somewhat calm, clenching his teeth and occasionally punching the side of his cot.

"What is your name sir?" she asked the man gently.

"I'm Private Bennings, ma'am." He could not have been much older than Alice. Cora nodded, taking his hand in hers.

"I am Cora Munro, it is very nice to meet you," she said.

"Munro? You're the colonel's daughter? Oh, I'm terribly sorry, ma'am, I can't s-stand...I can't bow... I'm awfully s-sorry," the man said, stumbling over his words.

"Shhh... no need," Cora soothed. "I am here to make you feel better and more comfortable. You are not required to give me my courtesies." She squeezed his hand.

"How old are you?" she asked.

"Eighteen, ma'am."

"That's a mighty smart age to be," she said, smiling down at him.

"I reckon it just might be the dumbest age to be! I volunteered to serve and here I am, eighteen years old and a cripple!"

"Shhh, that just means you made a great sacrifice to protect people like me. You are so brave, and all of Great Britain will thank you for it, starting with me." She squeezed his hand again.

He broke into a smile.

Alice was across the room, talking with a young man who had been shot in the abdomen. The surgeon had successfully extracted the bullet, but the man was still white-faced with pain. He could not have been more than sixteen.

He looked up at her when she came to stand next to him. His eyes were bloodshot from crying and Alice could see that his fists were clenched on the bed sheet that he was lying on.

"Are you an angel?" he asked her, entranced with the fair maiden's face.

Alice gave him a small smile and placed her hand on his shoulder gently.

"I am no angel, because you are still alive, and you will live," she urged him. "The surgeon has removed the bullet, and your bleeding has slowed." she said. This was true. His bleeding had slowed. However, he had lost far too much blood for him to recover.

"No need to give me false words of hope, miss. I am weak. I know I will not survive," he said through clenched teeth. "An angel you may not be, but I appreciate your sweetness, dear thing. It is a bit difficult, coming to terms with dying. If only I could hug my mama goodbye, ask my papa if he is finally proud of me. I am going to die, miss. I am going to die before I turn sixteen. I am going to die, bleeding, surrounded by smelly, d-dying men. Could I..." he hesitated. "C-Could you kiss me? I... I know it is an odd request, but I have never been kissed, and I do not want to go to my grave without k-knowing what it feels like..." he rambled.

Alice put a hand to his chest, feeling her own heart beating rapidly.

"It's going to be alright."

She looked down at the boy, fending off tears herself. She nodded slowly and lowered herself down to him, placing a small peck on his lips. He stared up at her and broke into tears. She grabbed his hands and held them, clasped together.

"May I pray for you?" she asked.

He nodded, his face contorting with both anguish and desperation.

"Lord Father, this man comes to you so young. He is a brave young man, and he is frightened to join you. Allow him peace as he takes the journey to be with you and walk by your side in paradise. Let him take these last few moments of his life for what they are; the transition between this mortal life of sin and pain and his life with you in Heaven," Alice said quietly, yet loud enough for the boy to hear.

She opened her eyes and kissed his hands, setting them back on the bed.

He looked up at her, his lips almost breaking into a smile.

"Bless you, ma'am. I will see you in paradise someday," he murmured, relaxing into the pillow as he closed his eyes for the last time. Alice rose from the side of the bed and wiped away tears before signaling the surgeon.

"Is he gone?" she asked, fighting her emotions.

The surgeon put his head to the man's chest and listened there for a minute. Then he rose to his feet and put his hand to his heart.

"Yes, ma'am, he is gone."

Alice dabbed at her eyes with a handkerchief. She stepped into the corner of the room to compose herself before she moved on to another soldier. The man was around thirty-five and had cuts and bruises all over his arms and face. He had been too near a wall hit by a cannon, and the debris had showered on him.

"And who are you, miss?" the man asked in a thicker Scottish accent than even their father had.

"I am Alice Munro, the colonel's daughter. What is your name, sir?"

"Corporal Alexander, ma'am, at your service," he said, raising his arm in the semblance of a courtly wave.

Alice smiled at his sense of humor in such circumstances.

"It is very nice to meet you, Corporal. Is there anything I can do to make you more comfortable?" The man was not in a dire condition, just a lot of pain.

"I s'pose there is. I'd think a pretty lass like yourself would be a singer?" he said.

Alice nodded. "I am, sir. Is there something you'd like to hear?"

"Aye. Do you know *I Once Loved a Lass*?" the man asked. Alice nodded and sat on the edge of the bed beside the man.

"*The week before Easter, the day being fair*
The sun shining brightly, cold frost in the air
I went into the forest some flowers to find there
And there I did pick my love a posy," she started, her voice a sweet melodic sound. The man closed his eyes and gave a contented sigh.

"Sing louder, lass! We canna hear ya over here!" one of the men on the other side of the room called out. Alice nodded and stood, continuing the song.

"*O I loved a lass and I loved her so well*
I hated all others who spoke of her ill
But now she's rewarded me well for my love
For she's gone and she's married another."

Cora walked over to join her sister, and she began singing the harmony of Alice's lines. The ladies' voices harmonized so beautifully that the men even stopped crying to listen to their song.

"*When I saw my love to the church go*
With bridesmen and bridesmaids she made a fine show
And I followed on with my heart full of woe
To see my love wed to another.
"*The parson who married them aloud he did cry*
All that forbid it I'd have you draw nigh
Thought I to myself I'd have a good reason why
Though I had not the heart to forbid it.
"*And when I saw my love sit down to meat*
I sat down beside her but nothing could eat
I thought her sweet company better than meat
Although she was tied to another.

"And when the bridesmaidens had dressed her for bed
I stepped in amongst them and kissed the bride
And wished that I could have been laid by her side
And by that means I'd got me the favour.
"The men in yon forest they are asking me
How many wild strawberries grow in the salt-sea
And I answer them back with a tear in my eye
How many ships sail in the forest.
"Go dig me a grave that is long, wide and deep
And cover it over with flowers so sweet
That I may lay down there and take a long sleep
And that's the best way to forget her.
"So they've dug him a grave and they've dug it so deep
And they've covered it over with flowers so sweet
And he has lain down there to take a long sleep
And maybe by now he's forgotten."

The ladies finished the song, and the men in the infirmary were quiet for some time, lying there with beatific smiles on their faces. The man that Alice was standing beside picked up her hand gently and laid a small kiss on it.

"Thank you, lass. That did more than ya could ever know," he said, smiling up at her.

Alice patted the man's hand, finally realizing the true cost of the war. Her father was a brave man, but who could be braver than these men here, who were dying for their country?

19
The Men's Opinions

18:09

"How long do you think the fort will last before surrendering?" Hawkeye asked his brother as he took a long drag of the pipe in his hand.

"Given the state that the fort is in now, I'd say not more than a week under siege, maybe nine days if they are smart about it."

Hawkeye shook his head as he blew out a cloud of smoke. "I don't think the fort will last a week, Uncas. Webb is not sending any relief, and the walls are practically crumbling now. Nobody can get in or out, so no food is going in. They cannot even get water from the lake now. Their supplies are running out fast. Soon Munro's hand will be forced."

"Mhm," Uncas said. "And when the fort does fall, what will happen to those inside?"

"Hopefully Munro has enough sense to surrender before the walls truly fall, or many more will die than necessary. If the Hurons and Ottawa get inside, they will slaughter all who remain. In the event

Munro surrenders, the survivors will likely march to Fort Edward," Hawkeye said.

"And the ladies, where will they go?" Uncas questioned, his voice light.

Hawkeye glanced at his brother, keeping his smirk at bay. "I am not sure, to be honest. Their father is growing old, so he may desire to retire and return to Scotland with his daughters."

"Return to Scotland? Are you sure they would want to go back? It seemed, despite their perilous journey, that the elder Miss Munro loves the countryside here in the Americas," Uncas said.

"Be that as it may, Scotland is their home. I understand you don't want her to leave Uncas. Believe me, I wish for them to stay as well, but the only reason the ladies would not follow their father is if they started a family of their own."

Uncas ran a hand over his face. "And do you think...Well, suppose they found someone in the Americas they wanted to make a life with? Do you think the men would be soldiers? Colonials? Indians?"

"If you are asking whether the eldest Miss Munro would be averse to marrying you because of your skin color, the answer is no. However, I do not know what lies in her heart, and if you want to know that, only she can tell you," Hawkeye said honestly.

"How could I ever go about asking her that? And..." Uncas' face fell, "...would father approve of such a marriage? She is not of our people, and my father has always said there is no point in me coupling." He looked down at his hands.

"In truth, I do not know what the sagamore would think. He may look favorably upon the match, due to your affections for the girl. But then again, she is no Mohican, and her marriage to you would not save your blood."

"But who could?" Uncas stood up and began to pace. "If no such women exist, why force myself into a life of celibacy, without love? Especially when there is a woman I have deep feelings for?"

"It is a good point. Perhaps you should ask Father," Hawkeye suggested. He knew that he could never understand Uncas' dilemma. Chingachgook would not care who Hawkeye decided to pair with, as his race was not dying.

8 August 1757

20
A Proposal
06:00

General Montcalm read over the dispatch again as he waited for Colonel Munro to arrive. If the meeting went well his men would be inside Fort William Henry within two days.

The flap of his tent was raised.

"Lieutenant Colonel George Munro and Major Duncan Heyward," his guard announced.

The men entered the tent, both wearing their dress uniforms, wigs and all. Munro stopped before the general and bowed, the major following his lead.

"General Montcalm, it is a pleasure to meet with you again. This is one of my field officers, Major Heyward."

The general nodded to the major, giving a polite smile.

"Ah, welcome in, Colonel Munro," the general said, his French accent butchering the words. "I am sure you know why I called you here?"

"I do, but my appearance here certainly does not signify my intention to surrender," Munro responded.

Montcalm chuckled at this comment. The Scottish man was always so defensive and prickly.

"Of course, Monsieur. However, it would be in your best interest to give up your defense of the fort and surrender. I understand there are women and children inside. In fact, it has reached my ears that your own daughters have recently arrived. You must know that were the walls of the fort to fall, I could not control everything my men or my Indian allies did in the breach. Many people could die, and I have no desire to see this happen to your women and children, Monsieur."

Munro's eyes flashed. "Sir, you intentionally laid your siege so it was impossible for me to get them out. I intended to have them all evacuated to Albany, but you made sure no one could get out of the fort without being taken by your men. Do not pretend that you care for my women and children!"

"Monsieur, you must know my siege of the fort would not be complete without cutting you off. If I had left a hole for women and children to escape, you may very well have used it for couriers or supplies. This is nothing personal, so please do not be offended."

Munro stood ramrod straight. "I am not offended, General. But I have no intention of surrendering this fort. I was given the orders to hold the fort and keep you from advancing toward Fort Edward, and that is what I will do," he said resolutely.

General Montcalm sighed.

"Very well, if this is how you want it," he said, motioning at one of his soldiers to come forward. The man was holding a tray, containing a white envelope with the seal broken.

Munro eyed it, his brows furrowing.

"This is a dispatch from General Webb. My men intercepted it this morning," Montcalm said, handing the dispatch to Munro.

Lieutenant Colonel George Munro,

I received your dispatch and I regret to inform you that I am unable to spare any troops or guns. Fort Edward needs every man it can get when

Montcalm inevitably gets through Fort William Henry and makes his way in our direction.

I understand that you have women and children in your fort. You cannot hope to stop the French with the limited men and resources at your disposal. You will be receiving no assistance from me. As for my instructions: you are to surrender the fort and bring your men here so that we might fight on when Montcalm attacks us here. Negotiate the best possible terms. I cannot imagine Montcalm would deny you full military honors, considering how long your fort has lasted under his siege guns.

I expect to see you in Fort Edward within the week.

General Daniel Webb

Montcalm watched Munro's fists clench as he finished reading the dispatch.

"Well sir, what is your conclusion? Will you listen to the calls of humanity?"

Munro handed the dispatch to Heyward, who scanned it.

The major looked up at Munro, then around the room. He took a step toward the colonel and leaned in close to whisper to him. Montcalm's lip curled up on one side as he listened to their quiet conversation.

"Are you sure this is authentic, sir? Could Montcalm not be trying to trick us into giving up the fort?" he asked.

"It's authentic. I have been staring at Webb's signature for some time now, I would recognize it anywhere."

Munro turned back to the general, drew himself up tall and lifted his chin.

"I will not surrender this fort unless it is my decision alone, I will not be pressured into it by my opponent!"

"But sir, does your commanding officer not order your surrender? Why are you so determined to keep this fort when you must know it is futile?"

"What I can and cannot do is none of your concern, sir! I demand twenty-four hours to confer with my officers before I give you a response."

The general sighed. "You may have your twenty-four hours, Colonel, but please, allow yourself to hear the cries of your wounded. Holding out would only hurt your reputation with your men."

"My reputation is none of your concern," Munro shot back. He bowed. "Good day to you, sir!"

The colonel turned on his heel and exited the tent, Major Heyward on his tail. Montcalm sat back down and put a hand to his temple.

Why is the colonel making this so much harder than it needs to be?

21
Officer Meeting

17:00

"Come in!" Munro called out. His deputy opened the door, and Munro's staff entered the meeting room. There were ten of them: captains, majors, and two lieutenant colonels. Their shoulders sagged, and their faces were tired and worn.

All the men greeted their commanding officer and stood behind their seats until Munro bade them to sit. Their eyes followed him, and Munro could see the concern etched into their faces. They knew why they were there.

"I am sure you have all deduced why you are here by now," he started. "We are besieged on all sides. General Montcalm has demanded my surrender, and General Webb has ordered it. This leaves me in an impossible position. I know that every man in this fort would go on fighting until the walls fell at our feet, but I am a soldier. I am required to follow the orders of my commanding officer. Gentlemen, I have to surrender. That being said, I will remain in this fort until Montcalm agrees to my terms!" the colonel announced.

"Hearing all of this, do you have any advice or opinions you wish to share with me? Know first, that I will hold nothing against any of you, and should there be reason for court martial for anyone's actions here,

I will tell my superiors that I ordered you to share your opinions," he prefaced.

"Permission to speak freely, sir?" Captain Sinclair said.

Munro nodded.

"Do you have the dispatch from General Webb?"

"No, General Montcalm kept it," Munro responded, already knowing where Sinclair was going with this.

"You never received the dispatch, then, sir! You do not have to obey the orders written in a dispatch you never received," Sinclair said.

Major Heyward leapt from his eat. "We did receive it. We do not have it, but we did receive it," he corrected him, glaring at the man. "If Webb ever questioned Montcalm, he would tell him that the colonel had seen the dispatch, and then what? We are not escaping our fate, and we are certainly not attempting to do it by besmirching the colonel's good name in the process!"

"Please sit down, Major Heyward," Munro said in a calm voice. He turned to the captain. "I have no intention of lying to my commanding officer, and I would advise you not to make such suggestions to me again. I appreciate how much you care for the continuation of the British presence on this lake, but I cannot allow my honor to come into question to stay here."

Sinclair looked at his hands but said nothing.

"Very well, if no one has any other *reasonable* suggestions, you may all go. I will be returning to inform General Montcalm that, under my conditions, I will surrender the fort. Have a good evening, gentlemen; go to your wives and enjoy your last night here in the fort."

22
The Officers' Wives

20:00

Cora tightened the laces of Alice's stays. Their father had given them brand-new dresses and instructed them to socialize with the officers' wives. There was sure to be a noticeable difference between officers' wives and enlisted men's wives.

Cora pulled on the beautiful golden dress, then Alice buttoned it up in the back for her. Afterward, Cora helped Alice put on her own sapphire blue dress, and the two examined themselves in the mirror. Alice sat in the chair in front of the mirror, and Cora began twisting her hair up into a complicated updo, ensuring that not a hair was out of place.

"Ow! Oh, that's too tight, Cora."

"I'm sorry, love. Father told us we should look as put together as possible. If we look in disarray, everyone will think he is, and that's bad for morale."

Alice nodded.

The ladies walked to the building, which was adjacent to the offi-cers' quarters. As the sisters walked inside, they noted the stark plainness of the room compared to the sitting rooms where they would normally enjoy such company. There were rustic-looking chairs and sofas, which had clearly been crafted here by the men of the fort. The walls had several paintings decorating it from the time before the siege, when the ladies were able to congregate there to knit, do needlepoint, and paint. During the siege, they had run out of supplies for such activities, so they would just amuse each other with music and poetry that they wrote.

Cora and Alice entered the room, smiling at the ladies around them. Alice smoothed her dress nervously as they reached the center of the room.

"My sister and I are so glad to officially meet you all!" Cora said. The ladies all began standing and making a circle around the Munro sisters, all very chipped and sweet.

"I am Hannah Kelly, Lieutenant Kelly's wife. It is such a pleasure to meet you, ladies!" the first girl said excitedly. She was around twenty and heavily pregnant. Cora and Alice both introduced themselves to her and then to the rest of the women, who were almost waiting in line to meet them.

"I am Billy!" a little boy said, running up to greet the Munro sisters. They gave him an odd look as they had not previously noticed the child. It seemed he had been hiding behind his mother's skirts. He bowed to Cora and Alice in turn, who both curtseyed back, laughing at the adorable little boy, who was no more than five.

The mother was very sweet, albeit a bit exhausted. Clearly, the woman had been focusing on watching her son while also supporting her husband's work. The woman was firm and yet very kind to the young boy, allowing him to run around with the other children of the ladies while the ladies entertained themselves, only stopping them if they became too loud. She occasionally brought a hand to her temple, grimacing.

"Alright, ladies, as you all know, our beautiful harpist, Deirdre, is going to perform for us tonight. After she is finished, we will have a poetry reading!" the woman who had introduced herself as Helen announced. The ladies all cheered as a young girl, no older than fourteen, approached the harp in the corner.

She took her seat and then all the ladies followed suit, finding some chair or sofa to sit on. Cora and Alice watched the girl crack her knuckles in preparation for the song. The ladies all watched in awe as the young girl began plucking the strings, fusing chords beautifully.

The song was very languid at first, just pretty chords strung together, but then the chords turned into a simple melody that rose and fell, telling a story of sorts. Deirdre was swaying with her music, her eyes closed. The girl was faultless, every note perfection.

The music began building until her fingers were weaving the notes and chords together so fast Alice could hardly make out which strings she was plucking. It all came to a head when she struck a powerful chord and then pulled back her hands to allow the strings to sing.

She held her hands there for a second, though done with her actual playing, waiting. Her eyes were still closed, as though she was cherishing every second of the beauty of her instrument. Once the chord had completely faded, the girl rose from her seat and stood beside the harp, grinning.

The ladies all erupted in applause. They stood up and hastened toward Deirdre, save Hannah, who remained seated with a hand on her belly.

"Beautiful, my dear!" Helen said.

"Breathtaking as always!" Hannah called from her seat.

The girl beamed and thanked the women for their praise. Cora squeezed her hand and smiled at her.

"You are so very talented, my dear. You should be performing in concert halls, not here in this fort."

The girl blushed.

"Thank you, ma'am. I love music for the joy it brings those who hear it, and who needs joy more than those in the middle of a war?" Cora's eyebrow raised at the comment, impressed with the emotional maturity of the young girl.

"Very well said, my dear."

"What a sweet angel you are," Helen said, standing from her chair. "Thank you, Deirdre." She turned to address the ladies. "Now, for our poetry reading, if anyone has something they would like to share, we can get started!"

An older woman rose and went to the front of the room, where she recited a short melancholic poem about the war stealing away young souls. The whole time, she tapped her feet, seemingly finding rhythm in her poetry and several of the women were brought to tears by this performance. Alice herself could feel the emotions welling up inside her as she applauded the woman's poem.

After the woman finished, Helen asked if anyone else wished to contribute. Alice bit her lip, unsure if she should share what she had written the night before. Cora saw the look on her face and urged her sister to rise and perform her poem. Her cheeks pink, the girl rose from her seat and made her way to the front of the room.

"My apologies if it isn't very good. I wrote it last night. I do not know what it means; something moved me to write it to write it, and I rather like what came out. I did not memorize it..."

"Memorization is not vital, my dear. It matters if it is from your heart," Helen replied.

Alice nodded, feeling more confident now. She stood with her hands loosely clasped in front of her.

"In quiet woods where shadows play,
A gentle heart, both wild and free,
He moves with grace through night and day,
A spirit bound by liberty.
"A steady hand, both firm and kind,
That guides with touch both soft and sure,
His voice, a solace to the mind,
Speaks truths that ever will endure.
"In him, the fire of courage burns,
A beacon in the darkest night,
Yet tenderness within him yearns,
A hidden, softly glowing light.
"A man of earth, of wind and trees,
Of rivers wide and mountains high,
His presence, like a summer breeze,
Unseen, but felt, when he is nigh.
"I dream of him, this noble soul,
Whose heart beats with the wild and free,
For I know not who'll fill this role,
I only know he's made for me."

All the women just stared at her in awe for a second. A few of their mouths even dropped open. Alice bit her lip, awaiting their reaction.

"Alice, that was amazing! Who is this dear spirit?" one girl asked.

"Is it a soldier here?" another questioned.

"Oh my, you must tell us who it is! He sounds amazing!" Hannah said, clasping her hands together over her heart.

"Oh, but he is no one, really. Just something that came to me, a man my heart desires, undoubtedly, but a man of my imagination," Alice explained, staring at her hands.

"The young Miss Munro desires a woodsy man. How romantic!" one of the younger ladies exclaimed.

Alice blushed, not knowing how to respond. The poem had truly felt like it came to her from nothing, but they were right that it described a type of man she had not encountered before coming to the Americas.

"Maybe someday I will have an answer for you all," Alice said. Cora took her sister's hand, a small smirk playing on her lips, and led Alice to the door.

"Thank you all so much for allowing us to join you today. Hopefully, we will be able to attend tomorrow as well. Helen, thank you for being such a gracious host. Have a lovely night!" Cora said, curtsying to the room of ladies. Alice followed suit, and the two walked out to head back to their room.

"Flower, that was beautiful. You continue to amaze me with your talent!" Cora praised her sister.

Alice beamed, not knowing how to respond to the compliment. She could only think about the poem she had written and what had inspired her to write such a thing. She grasped the paper that it was penned on tightly in her hand as the two of them entered their room to prepare for bed.

9 August 1757

23
Surrender Negotiations - 06:00

C olonel Munro walked into the now-familiar white tent of General Montcalm, his face a mask of the perfect soldier, stoic and expressionless, while he screamed in his head. The general was smirking at Munro, which made him want to slap the man, but he restrained himself, clenching his jaw and bringing his hands behind his back to hide his balled fists.

Munro removed his hat and tucked it close to his chest as he bowed to the general, Major Heyward following his lead behind him. "Good morning, General."

The general returned the bow, sweeping his arm flamboyantly. "Good morning, Monsieur. Have you come to a decision?"

Munro held in the bitter comment that he so desperately wanted to make.

"I have."

"Well, do you intend to make me guess, Monsieur?"

"I will yield my fort to you…"

The general broke into a grin.

"...if, and only if we receive full military honors consistent with the valor with which we have opposed your forces," Munro finished.

Montcalm's face dropped ever so slightly, but he quickly recovered. "Why of course, Monsieur. You have fought most valiantly, and your king should be very proud. We shall proceed as follows: You will get full military honors. You shall also keep your arms, though I will have to take your ammunition supply. You may load your guns before you leave, but no other powder or lead may go with you. You may keep your colors and carry them back to England with pride. Finally, you may keep one cannon of your choosing. Monsieur, my field doctors will tend to all of your sick and wounded using our own supplies; you will just need to let them into the fort. I will allow all of this, but you and your men must return to England and not fight for eighteen months. I'm sure you can understand, Monsieur. I do not wish to take this fort only to face the same men later on in this campaign."

Munro glanced back at Major Heyward, and the two shared a knowing look. They both knew good and well that all the men leaving Henry would go straight to Fort Edward to defend it when Montcalm traveled further south.

Turning back to Montcalm, the colonel said, "Very well, I surrender my fort to you under these terms, sir. We shall depart from the fort at 07:30 tomorrow morning. I will spend the day preparing my people to leave, and I would ask that you send in your doctors and supplies as soon as possible. The fort is now yours, so the gate will remain open so that you might come and go as you please. Your doctors may use this to assist my wounded, and should you need to contact me, you may come straight to me instead of sending a party to retrieve me. I will ensure that all the ammunition in the fort, save what is in my men's guns, as well as the powder and the cannons, is all locked up tonight.

Sir, it has been a pleasure meeting you; I only wish it could be under different circumstances."

"Likewise," Montcalm responded.

Munro bowed to his adversary, and Montcalm returned the gesture. Then Munro and Heyward exited the tent and mounted their horses to make the trip back to the fort.

24
The Fort's
Surrender - 15:00

Colonel Munro stood atop the parapet, wearing his dress uniform complete with a powdered wig. He gazed down at all the people gathered in the square of the fort. It still shocked him that so many people could fit into such a small space. There were around 2,500 people in total, mostly soldiers and colonial militiamen, but there were women and children too, the families of those soldiers. The soldiers ranged from young men who couldn't grow a beard to old hardened war veterans who were all gray.

The people were all staring up at him expectantly, waiting for what he would say. He lifted his pocket watch, eyeing the hands moving along slowly, and when it struck 15:00, he began his speech.

"Men, ladies, and of course, children, I have met with Montcalm to discuss our fort's future. He has requested my surrender on the grounds of..." Munro swallowed. "...humanity. I am sure most of you have been wondering about our relief. Where are the men that General Webb has sent? I will answer you now; they are not coming. General Webb has received our courier and has responded. I did not receive his word because the Hurons had been...intercepting them. I am a soldier, an officer of His Majesty's service. I must show respect to my superiors, even when they *do not* deserve it," Munro bit his lip to keep in his thoughts. "General Webb has informed me that we will not be receiving his assistance."

Murmurs rippled through the crowd below. The colonel paused to allow the crowd to make their comments. "He has also ordered me to surrender." The crowd of soldiers and colonials erupted into shouts at this, everyone giving their opinion at once. When the colonel held up his hand, they all respectfully quieted. "I would fight to hold this fort until they burned it to the ground, despite my orders, if I knew that only those in His Majesty's service would perish. However, General Montcalm predicted this. He is aware that he will need all his men to take Fort Edward, and he cannot waste them fighting here. He has surrounded our fort, which makes it impossible for our women and children to escape. He has forced my hand by threatening them. This is why I must..." Munro swallowed again, his voice hard and emotionless. He winced, his head pounding, and closed his eyes for a second before continuing. "... surrender." The crowd erupted again, everyone giving their opinions to their neighbors.

Munro waited for them to quiet before he went on. "This agreement was made this morning, and we have received a promise of full military honors.[1] Montcalm has allowed us to keep our guns and our colors, and a single canon, provided we all leave this country and do not fight again in this theatre." The soldiers all chuckled a bit here. Of course, they would not return to England, not with Fort Edward so close and in need of help soon. Munro continued. "We will be leaving the fort tomorrow morning and marching to Fort Edward. Please spend the rest of the day packing and readying yourselves for the journey. I will leave you with this; I thank all of you for your outstanding defense of this fort, and I am so sorry that I could not do more to keep it."

The crowd all began discussing this resolution, as the colonel stepped down from the parapet to join his daughters in the adjoining room.

---

1. Full military honors were granted when the victorious commander believed the surrendering commander had put up a valiant fight. An army could be refused these honors if the victorious commander believed the army gave up too easily. General Montcalm denied a British commander full honors exactly a year before he granted Munro full honors. Full honors generally included marching out with flags flying and having bayonets fixed, as well as being able to play music of their choice.

25

The Ladies'
Opinions - 17:12

Alice was sitting at her desk, thumbing through her Bible, when she heard a knock on her door. She put the Bible down and walked over to the bed to begin packing, as she should have already been doing.

"Come in!" she shouted. The door opened, and Cora walked in. Alice smiled at her sister.

"Come now, Alice, I know you were not packing. Sit and let us talk," Cora said, taking a seat on the edge of their bed. Alice joined her and Cora took up her sister's hand in her own.

"Do you know what tomorrow will bring, flower?" Cora asked.

"I suppose we will just march to Fort Edward. What else will happen?"

"Well, there will be an official ceremony for Father to hand the fort over to General Webb, and then, yes, we will walk to Fort Edward. This will take a long time because of all the wounded needing transport. We will be on our feet for around eight hours, although we will likely take a break to eat and rest. And the French...they might burn the fort, I am not sure about that, but Papa mentioned they intend to destroy it."

Alice paused for a second, biting her lip, but eventually she asked the question that was on her mind.

"Cora, do you think it might have been better for us to stay at Fort Edward? Our journey has been perilous and deadly. Two men died because we decided to come here, and that's not even counting the Hurons..." Alice almost burst into tears at the thought of poor Hector lying on the ground, blood pouring from his chest. He was a good man, and he had died trying to protect them.

"This only happened because of the siege of the fort, which we could not have possibly known about," Cora reassured her. "It was very dangerous, but we got through, and we are with Father now. You know he is not a young man anymore, dear sister. If we had waited back at Fort Edward or Albany, perhaps we would have received word that our father had died, and we would not have seen him for a decade."

Alice nodded, understanding. They were both silent for a second, enjoying the quiet that the ceasefire had brought. Alice finally decided to break the silence.

"You haven't stopped thinking about him, have you?" she questioned, knowing that her sister would understand her meaning. Sure enough, Cora's eyes widened and her cheeks turned bright red.

"How did you know?"

"Please, you are my sister! I have never seen you look at a man the way you looked at him, Cora."

"Oh, well I suppose that is true. I have never met a man like him before," she admitted. "You will not tell Papa, will you?"

"Of course not, but if you love Uncas and have any desire to marry him, you are going to have to tell Father eventually," Alice pointed out.

Cora nodded.

"Have you decided what it is that *you* want in a man?" Cora questioned, redirecting the conversation. Alice smirked, knowing what her sister was doing.

"I have. Being here in the Americas has made me realize what I disliked about the perfect soldier archetype. I must marry a man who is brave and strong. A man who can protect me," Alice started.

"Like Duncan?" Cora teased. Alice's face got red and her eyes bulged.

"Major Heyward? Certainly not." Alice dabbed at her mouth with a handkerchief, her other hand pressed to her chest. "I must marry a man who respects me; one who can protect me but does not treat me as though I were incompetent or childish. And it would be nice if he cared about my interests. I have no desire to hear boast after boast. If a man must tell me he is great, he must not truly be that great!" the girl announced to her sister.

Cora grinned. "Ah, I see. I know exactly what kind of man you want. A man whose name alone draws fear? I know what man would be right for you!"

"You do? Tell me!" Alice demanded, giggling.

"Of course not, flower! You must figure that out on your own!" Cora said playfully. Alice groaned, protesting this, but her sister gave no answer, and the two laughed together through the night as they readied themselves for the journey ahead.

26
Night in the Infirmary - 22:13

S pirits were high in the infirmary that evening. Montcalm, true to his word, had sent his surgeons with supplies, and all of Munro's men received treatment at once, instead of having to wait to see the single English surgeon who had been caring for all of them, rushing from soldier to soldier, barely getting a moment to rest.

That afternoon, many more of the soldiers' wives had offered to act as nurses for the surgeons than usual, and a few of the officers' wives had joined Cora and Alice in visiting to sing to the men. The men clapped along to the women's songs and cheered when they finished each one.

Hannah Kelly had gone into labor, and she was in an alcove in the corner, separated by a curtain. Every few seconds, the men's attention would be drawn away from the singing to the screams of the woman, but in between cries and deep breaths, she encouraged them to enjoy their night and the chance for some relaxation.

When it was time for supper, most of the ladies, save Hannah and a few nurses, left. The surgeons returned to the French camp, leaving the English surgeon and nurses to care for the men overnight. The men hummed some of the tunes the ladies had sung, and a few played cards. They were relieved they were finally able to have some peace.

That was, until dusk. Soon, darkness fell on the infirmary, and with it came the natives. Around a dozen natives entered the fort at dusk and found their way into the infirmary.

Corporal Alexander was the first to see them. An Ottawa warrior peered in through the window. Alexander did a double take when he saw him, and he nudged the soldier beside him, pointing at the window.

The Ottawa threw the door open and took in all the terrified wounded who began screaming when they saw him. He let out a fierce yell and then rushed inside. Twelve other natives, from varying tribes that supported the French, followed him in, knives and hatchets glinting in the candlelight. The last warrior inside, an Abenaki, stood in the doorway.

Screams rang out as the soldiers realized what was happening, and the men who could get to their feet tried to fight. None of the soldiers were armed; they grabbed anything they could find to fend off the natives. The warriors descended on the soldiers, cutting through most of them easily.

The few nurses who had stayed behind shrieked, running for corners and seeking places to hide. One ran for the door, seeing it to be open. The Abenaki met her there. She screamed, realizing her mistake, and turned to escape. He grabbed her wrist, pulling her back to him, as he embedded his knife into her chest. The fortunate woman died almost as soon as she hit the ground, which spared her the horror of feeling her scalp sliced from her head.

The surgeon, who had been assisting Hannah, rushed out from behind the curtain, pulling it shut to conceal his patient.

"What in God's name—" He was interrupted by a thrown hatchet, which split his skull, leaving the contents of his head decorating the floor around him where he fell.

The men in the infirmary fought with everything they could, wielding chairs like clubs. They had managed to create a circle around the few nurses who remained alive, but this left the infirm, bedridden soldiers completely helpless. The warriors went around, sinking their knives into these men's chests, who could do nothing but scream and watch the natives advance on them.

Once all the bedridden were dead, the natives turned on the circle protecting the women. The warrior's knives became projectiles and cut down several of the men. On threw his hatchet right at Alexander's face, but the man was quick enough to block it with his chair. The force of the throw threw him to the ground, but the chair slowed it enough to just barely break the skin. Alexander pushed the chair off himself, trying to rise to his feet.

A Wendat in the corner tore aside the curtain that had served as Hannah's shield. She sobbed, one hand on her belly, the other clutching the sheets of the bed she lay on.

"Please..." she begged before screaming as another contraction ripped through her body.

The Wendat examined her for a second, bringing his bloody hand to her belly and laying it atop her own hand. Her hand was tensed up from the pain of the contraction, and as it ended, he felt her hand ease up.

He removed his hand, taking a step back. She looked up at him, her eyes pleading. He said something in Wyandot and closed the curtain, leaving her to her own fight.

Corporal Alexander looked around, realizing all his comrades had fallen. He turned to see two natives already descending on the remaining nurses. The room was filled with the screams of frightened females and the stink of the blood that pooled on the floor. He looked up to see three warriors approaching him, and he cursed at them, grabbing a broken table left on the ground and holding it up to defend himself.

The warriors disarmed the corporal in seconds; then one plunged his knife into the man's gut. Howling in agony, Alexander dropped the table leg, bringing his hands down to the wound. He fell to his knees, muttering under his breath. "Our Father, who art in Heaven, hallowed—"

A Shawnee grabbed him by his hair, and Alexander flailed at the man, trying to push him away. However, the Shawnee brought his knife to the edge of Alexander's hairline.

"Be damned!" Alexander shouted as the Shawnee drug his knife below the layer of skin atop Alexander's head, slicing off his scalp. Alexander's world erupted into pain as he fell against the floor, his body convulsing in shock. Blood flowed from his head as his eyes wavered, determined to stay open as long as possible.

So they've dug him a grave and they've dug it so deep
And they've covered it over with flowers so sweet
And he has lain down there to take a long sleep
And maybe by now he's forgotten

27
Repercussions
22:57

"How many?" Munro asked Captain Watts, looking upon the carnage of the Infirmary, a kerchief pressed to his nose. He reached out to support himself on the doorframe. Dead soldiers and nurses covered the floor and the beds. The infirmary had already stunk of blood before the attack, but now it was overwhelming.

The corpses seemed thrown about, discarded by an uncaring enemy. Many of them still wore faces of terror. Everyone had been scalped, but some had no wounds other than those atop their heads. The colonel, though a hardened war veteran, felt sick to his stomach knowing that his men had died like that: bleeding to death from the natives' attack.

Amidst all the death and destruction, Munro could hear the frightened cries of a baby. He stepped over the scalped bodies and pulled aside the curtain to reveal Hannah, clutching her child to her chest. Her hair stuck to her face and neck with sweat and she sat in a mess of blood and other bodily fluids. She was sobbing and rocking back and forth. Munro put a hand on her shoulder to steady and calm her.

"All the men that were in here have perished. Those monsters spared none but I," she said through her tears.

"Twenty-six men, four women," Captain Watts reported.

Munro was struggling to maintain his composure. Montcalm was responsible for keeping his men at bay, but he had failed to stop them from killing his most helpless people.

"You have to get justice for them, sir," the woman begged, using her free hand to grab his coat. "They died in anguish and with no hope. No men deserve to go that way," she said. Munro nodded and held her hand in his.

"I will bring the men that did this to justice, Hannah. They will pay, I swear it." She nodded, taking him at his word. Munro turned to his deputy and instructed the man to make all arrangements for the woman and child to be taken care of and then he left the Infirmary.

The colonel did not even bother retrieving Duncan or any of his other officers. This meeting would be conducted by him alone. He stalked through the open gates that had allowed the natives to enter the fort and began his walk across the bridge to the French pickets.

The Frenchmen who saw Munro coming gave him wary looks and tried to avoid eye contact. He was bright red with an expression that could kill.

"I demand to speak to General Montcalm!" Munro shouted in Corporal Serre's face. The man bit his lip, but kept an otherwise neutral expression.

"I am afraid the general is very busy. He will not be able to talk with you right now," Serre said.

"Well make time, dammit! I demand to speak with him now!"

Serre shook his head. "Sir, I will not be disturbing my master's work for you. I suggest you return to the fort."

Colonel Munro raised an eyebrow at the audacity of the man.

"Oh, I see! You think that because I have surrendered it means you can tell ME what to do? I am a lieutenant colonel, and you are a foot soldier who has been lucky enough to wipe the general's arse! I WILL speak to him! NOW!"

"The general will speak with you tomorrow during the official surrender of the fort." Serre repeated in a calm voice. "I have nothing further to say to you, sir. You may leave, or the men will have to escort you back."

Munro seethed, clenching his fists. He might not have been the most decorated officer, but he was an officer, and he'd be damned if he let some corporal tell him what to do. He put a finger in the young man's face and wagged it about.

"I am leaving now, but I will talk to your master of your disrespect tomorrow morning. I will not rest until they demote you at least or discharge you at most!" Munro said, spinning on his heel and stomping his way back to the fort.

28
The Men's Conversation

23:24

U ncas and Hawkeye sat in the cave at Glen, waiting for their father to return with the berries he had set out to gather. They cooked some venison over the small fire they had made, keeping it just low enough that the smoke would be minimal.

"What are you thinking about, brother?" Hawkeye questioned. Uncas had been staring at the wall for a few minutes now, seemingly lost in his thoughts. He looked up and saw Hawkeye's knowing grin.

"I, just...What if I never see her again?" he asked. "Nineteen years and I have never met a woman like her before. She is so kind, and wise, and so beautiful. I do not think I could stand going the rest of my life without knowing what she would say if I told her..."

"That you love her," Hawkeye finished his sentence, realizing that the feelings Uncas had were real, not just some attraction, but an honest desire to be with the woman. Uncas grinned.

"I love her, you are right!" he said, leaping to his feet. "Hawkeye, I love her and I cannot bear the thought of not seeing her again. I will visit her at Fort Edward! The fort on the lake has been yielded to the French. They will all be marching to Fort Edward, very likely tomorrow morning. I will meet Cora there and tell her how I feel!" Uncas said, hugging his brother.

Hawkeye looked down at his younger brother, half in amusement, half in shock. He had assumed that Uncas had feelings for the girl; his eyes got stars in them whenever he saw her, but Hawkeye had not realized the depths of Uncas' affections. The pair had spent a good amount of time talking in the cave, so it made sense, but it was still shocking nonetheless. Uncas had never had feelings for a woman before.

"Very well, I will come with you," Hawkeye said.

"You will?" Uncas questioned. "For what reason? I had assumed you would disapprove of my feelings. Cora Munro is not a Delaware, and was that not your plan for me?"

"Certainly not, brother. I wish only for you to be happy. I thought marrying a Delaware might make this possible."

"You wish me happiness?" Uncas asked, laughing at his brother's comment.

"Of course, just so long as I am happier. I cannot have you beating me in that race, brother," Hawkeye laughed and ruffled Uncas' hair.

"Besides," Hawkeye said, bringing the conversation back to the journey to Fort Edward. "I have my own reasons to go as well." He gave a mysterious smile.

Uncas raised a brow, turning on his brother.

"Have you?"

"That is *all* you will get out of me," Hawkeye said, chuckling and swatting away Uncas' attempts to put him into a choke hold.

10 August 1757

29
Trŭcīdo

07:30

The official surrender was over in mere minutes and with few words. Munro attempted to speak with Montcalm, but the man did not respond, ignoring everything the colonel said until he moved on from the topic. Munro seethed, but he was at the general's disposal. So there was nothing to be done.

The occupants of the fort began their slow march toward Fort Edward. All the men marched in their columns, their loaded arms on their shoulders. The women and children all walked beside a wagon carrying food and other supplies that had been scarce in the fort before the surrender.

Cora pulled her shawl back up onto her shoulders. The crowd exiting the fort amounted to over two thousand. All the men kept their military bearing as they marched out, their faces emotionless, but the women and colonials stared at the ground as they walked. Everyone was solemn and quiet. Alice's arm wrapped around Cora's and Cora stroked Alice's hand gently to soothe her.

"Do you know yet, will they burn the fort, Cora?" Alice asked.

Cora gave her sister a small smile.

"I don't know, flower. It is possible, but they may want to keep it for themselves."

Billy ran around the group of colonials marching. His mother chased him, trying to convince him to save his energy for the long march down the wagon road. He locked eyes with the younger Miss Munro, and Alice smiled at him, giving a small wave.

Cora looked ahead at the group of officers who rode in front of the colonials. Heyward rode a horse out beside her father. Cora noted that every couple of seconds the young major turned his head and looked at her sister.

The ladies trudged along, unconsciously walking in beat with the drum that the men marched to. Cora's eyes flew around, taking everything in. The first time she had been out here, the fort was under siege. It seemed as though she was constantly in danger.

As they got further and further from the fort, the group noticed natives standing on the edge of the path. At first, there was only one every couple of yards, but the farther the inhabitants of the fort traveled, the more there were. They were Wendats, Ottawa, Abenaki, and Nipissing. Alice gripped Cora's arm, terror striking her gentle form.

"Cora..." Alice whispered.

"What's wrong, my flower?"

"Something's wrong... Why are they..." Alice stuttered, "Magua," she said, finally noticing Le Renard Subtil standing with his brethren. He looked somewhat different now from how he had when they were his prisoners. He had added red feathers to his hair, and painted the bottom half of his face red.

The party slowed to a halt as the wheel of the supply wagon had jammed between two rocks. Cora stiffened when she noticed *Le Renard*'s stare. His eyes bore into her, cutting through her like the knife with which he fought. Cora moved around Alice, keeping her sister on the inside, putting herself in between her sister and those who might harm her. She shot a look toward Billy and his mother to ensure that he was safe with his mother and not running about as he had been.

Billy stood by his mother's side, his arms wrapped around her leg as he stared out at the Wendats, eyes wide with fear. Billy's mother had a bright orange shawl wrapped around her shoulders, protecting her exposed neck from the heat and wind. One of the Wendats took a few steps toward the woman, eyeing the shawl with hungry eyes.

The mother watched him cautiously, keeping a firm grip on Billy's wrist. He hid between her legs, eyes locked on the interloper. The Wendat took another step forward so that he was within arm's reach of the terrified mother. Her lip quivered, and her eyes followed every motion he made.

He reached a steady hand forward and sought purchase on the orange shawl. She gripped it by the edge and tried pulling away from him. "Let go! Leave me be!" she shouted at him, slapping at his hand, which held firm on the clothing article.

The Wendat released the shawl, as she requested, but grabbed young Billy by his short ponytail instead, pulling him up by his hair.

Billy squealed. "Mama, make it stop! He's hurting me!"

The mother screamed and pulled the shawl from her shoulders.

"No! No! Take it! Please! Anything, take any of my possessions, but return me my child!" she cried out, throwing the shawl at him. She fell to her knees and clamped her hands together, begging him.

"Mama!" Billy cried out, still thrashing around in the Wendat's grasp. Cora paled, and she began pulling Alice away from the group, moving to hide behind the stuck wagon. The Wendat released Billy's hair and wrapped his hands around his waist. The mother calmed for a brief second, believing this to be mercy. The Wendat raised the young boy up and then slammed him back to the ground, dashing his head against a large rock.

Screams erupted from the onlooking crowd as the blood from Billy's cracked skull flowed down the side of the rock. His mother's cry dissolved into wails of anguish as she threw herself upon her lost son's body, trying in vain to stir him. The Wendat called out a war cry and embedded his hatchet in the mother's head.

Shouts and cries sounded from the people in the crowd as the natives descended on the colonials. The men tried to pull their ranks together and fight, but it was so chaotic they were scarcely able to tell which direction the enemy came from. With only one round in each gun, the men had very little to fight with and were left to take on the advancing natives hand to hand.

Some of the colonials tried to fight, but there was only so much they could do against a far larger force. Around four thousand natives descended on the party. The women all began scattering, trying to run away, but many were chased down and killed, or tied up and carried away as trophies of the battle. Most of the men who discharged their shots suffered the same fate; either a hatchet in their chest or dragged away as captives.

Cora held Alice in her arms, keeping her back to the wagon in an effort to protect them from a surprise rear attack. Many natives saw the two of them but seemed to ignore them, turning and running off to kill others. David stayed by their side, his voice ringing out in a psalm. The natives would pause briefly, watching him with wide eyes, before running away and attacking someone else.

Seeing Magua approaching them out of the corner of her eye, Cora let out a guttural sob. The villain was clearly involved in the attack to recapture them. She searched around for her father, Duncan, or anyone who might protect them from the man.

Magua smirked upon seeing her realization.

"Come on, my flower, we need to get away!" Cora shouted to her sister over the sounds of muskets firing and the screams of the fallen.

She dragged Alice away from him, trying to stay near the wagon. Magua rushed toward them. David stood in his way, keeping the women behind him, but Magua easily slung him aside.

"Leave her be, Huron!" David yelled, surprising the ladies by standing up to someone for what seemed like the first time. The psalmodist was obviously brave, but he had never seemed the outspoken type. Magua turned on him, bearing his knife.

"The others may see your obvious madness as something to be feared, but I do not. Stand in my way, and I will kill you!" Magua threatened. Shaking his head, David took a step forward, but Cora shoved him away, not wanting him to be hurt on her behalf.

"You will come with me, Cora," Magua said, grabbing her by the wrist. She wrenched her arm free and pulled away from him.

"Never!" Magua tried pulling her again, but she had an iron grip on the wagon's edge with her other arm. He glared at her and growled something under his breath. She saw an idea dawn on him, and before she could react, he grabbed Alice by the wrist and slung her over his back.

Cora shouted, pulling at Alice's arm as her little sister screamed. "Stop, you evil man! Let her go!" However, Magua walked off with Alice over his shoulder, pulling out of Cora's grasp with ease. Cora chased after them, begging David to follow. Magua led them off toward the woods.

As she ran, Cora watched other natives dragging along their own captives, some men, some women, no children. Tears fell down her face as she saw all the dead sprawled along the path. Neither her father nor Heyward was in sight.

As the ladies disappeared with Magua, the English infantrymen began to regroup and were starting to pull together to repel the attack. After they had successfully dwindled the natives' numbers down enough they began to escape, making a forced run to Fort Edward. At this point, all the women and children were either dead or in the hands of the natives.

Some distance from this all, Chingachgook, Hawkeye, and Uncas were breaking their fast together on some fish Uncas had caught. The gunshots from the attack ripped through the air and reached the ears of the men. They all shot to their feet, without words, and raced toward the fort, knowing that was the only place it could have come from.

By the time the men reached the path that the colonials and soldiers had taken, there were nary twenty natives left, although at this point all but Major Heyward and Colonel Munro had deserted. The three men each shot a man and then Uncas began picking off the rest of the natives with his bow. Chingachgook dove into the heat of the battle, chopping away at his adversaries with his hatchet.

The colonel and Heyward hardly had time to acknowledge the men's help, as they were each fighting with everything in them to stay alive. Hawkeye took shot after shot, picking up guns from dead soldiers, hoping they hadn't been fired before their owners fell.

But eventually, all the natives were dead. The colonel was running around checking bodies, calling out his daughters' names with a desperation that could only have come from a father. Uncas started searching the carnage, his eyes peeled for a certain black-haired woman. Of course, she was nowhere to be found.

"Cora!" Uncas called, his voice breaking in desperation. The colonel's gaze was fixed on the young Mohican, his expression darkening.

30
Lake Champlain

08:12

M agua did not put Alice down until they reached the canoes at the lake. At that point, his men dragged Cora into one of the canoes and then placed Alice in another. David slipped into an open spot at the back of the younger sister's canoe. Rolling his eyes at the psalmodist, Magua boarded behind Cora and immediately began paddling after the canoe was pushed into the water.

Alice looked over at her sister, her eyes tearing up. Cora nodded back, mouthing to her that everything would be alright. They glided along, as three of the five men in each canoe were paddling hard.

The fort receded into the distance as they traveled up Lake George, and Alice began softly weeping as she watched it get smaller. The girl wondered if she would ever see her father, or the Mohicans ever again. Magua was taking them north; if they crossed the border into Canada they would be in Huron country, and she could not be saved.

"Why do you cry? Can the white woman not take responsibility for her actions?" the man behind her questioned in French. Alice snapped her head around to look at him. He was maybe two years her senior, and his face was soft, with a hooked, eagle-like nose that made him look regal.

"My actions? What have I done to warrant this?" she responded through tears.

"Your people have come to drive us away; our Canadian fathers would let us keep our land![1] "

"Very well, I cannot disagree with this assertion. I am truly sorry that this has happened to your people, but I am not to blame. I have only just arrived here, and my sister and I were to return to the land we came from; we had no intention of staying here and keeping your land for ourselves," Alice explained.

"But you are the seed of he who would. The gray-haired colonel on the lake would take our land. Are you not his kin?"

"Aye, we are, but shall we answer for the crimes of our father?" she asked.

The young man was silent for a moment.

"No, I suppose you should not. But Magua does not give us meaningless orders. He is a great chief," he asserted.

Alice bit her lip.

"Magua is a great leader, I cannot deny this, but was it not Magua who led forty of your men to their deaths at Glen?" she pushed. The man's chin rose.

"Those men died heroes. It would be a great honor to die for my chief."

Alice nodded, clasping her hands.

---

1. Save the Iroquois Confederacy, essentially every tribe supported the French during the French and Indian War. This was because the French allowed them more access to their land, whereas the English were much more brutal and caused a lot of problems for the Native Americans.

"I understand that, I am Scottish. We tried fighting off the British ten years ago. We didn't succeed, but the men who died then are heroes to us. Would a great chief not have realized how meaningless that attack was? Did Magua tell you he was attacking to kill *La Longue Carabine*, or did he tell you the truth?"

"What truth?"

"Magua attacked Glen to capture me and my sister. He wanted to take his revenge for my father's actions with us. He wishes to marry my sister. How could you defend that?"

"I... I suppose it is odd that he would risk so many of our lives to take his revenge on some women..." the man started.

"I would call it reckless," Alice retorted. "Should a chief be reckless?"

Realization dawned in the man's eyes. "You are trying to convince me to help you!"

Alice put a hand on the man's forearm, looking up at him through her long, doe-like lashes. "I am only showing you the truth of the man you follow; anything you do as a result is your decision," she whispered back. "What, pray tell, is your name?"

"Teharihoyen," the man said.

"I am Alice Munro. I am not telling you to do anything; just try to understand what your *chief* has put me and my sister through," she said.

Teharihoyen looked at her with stony eyes before shaking his head fervently.

"No... no... I cannot... I will not..." he began muttering to himself.

Alice nodded, giving him a small frown before turning back to the front and smirking to herself. The seed was planted.

31
Discussion and Disagreement

10:12

The men searched the carnage for hours to find the ladies. It was a horrible sight; the path was littered with the dead from Fort William Henry. There were so many women and children; it made Munro sick to his stomach to see it. He should have known that Montcalm would allow such villainous behavior to occur after the events in the infirmary the day before.

The natives had left nothing but destruction in their wake. They had massacred everyone they could before they were called away, and even then, they took some of the colonials and soldiers captive for ransom purposes.

Of course, the Munro sisters' bodies were nowhere to be seen on the path. They were fortunate to survive but at the cost of falling back into Magua's hands.

"Did you find anything? Even a clue that my daughters survived?" Munro demanded of Hawkeye, who was conversing with his family in Algonquian.

"They're alive, Colonel. Magua wanted Cora, so he would have certainly taken her captive. Alice was either taken as a prisoner for ransom or as a way to coerce Cora into following him," Hawkeye explained.

"I believe it to be the latter," Uncas added. "Magua was carrying one of the sisters, and I believe Cora would have been able to put up more of a fight if he had tried to pick her up."

"Are you suggesting my Alice has no fight?" Munro questioned, his pride hurt.

"Of course not, Colonel. Only I have seen Cora kill a man; her stomach is not turned by blood or violence the way your younger daughter's is," Uncas replied.

Munro glared at the man but gave no response to this.

"So you saw their tracks? You know where they went?" Munro demanded.

"Yes," Uncas replied.

"Tell me where they went, so I may find them!"

"Sir, with respect, you are going to need our help," Uncas argued. "We have been further north than you, we know the lands, and we know the ways that Magua will try to throw you off."

"I will not accept help from savages like you!" Munro shouted. "Your people are the very ones who attacked us to begin with!"

"How dare you! My family has done nothing but help and rescue yours, and you would call me and my son savages?" Chingachgook demanded, taking a step forward.

"No, I would call you and your *sons* savages, brutal men that live off the land and have no honor or rank!" he replied.

"Oh, the honor it must require for you to spit in the face of those who delivered your daughters to safety!" Hawkeye retorted, coming to stand next to his father.

Major Heyward put a hand in between the men and turned to look at the colonel.

"Sir, please, for the sake of your daughters, can you put this aside and allow these men to help us? They know what they are doing!"

"Oh, you think we are here to offer our help now?" Hawkeye demanded. "Your colonel has just insulted us, and you think we desire to help you any longer? Certainly not! I am not here to be the slave of the Munro family! We will rescue your daughters, but for their sake, not yours, and I pray that we never see you again, sir!" Hawkeye spat the word in his face.

"Brother," Uncas said, grabbing Hawkeye and pulling him back from the decorated man. "He is a grieving father. I am sure he is just distressed from the events that have occurred."

Colonel Munro bit his tongue, wanting to claim this statement false. But instead, he slowly nodded. "I am... sorry. I must a-apologize... My behavior was unacceptable," he managed to get out. "I would be most grateful if you would help us find and recover my daughters."

"Very well, let us be off then!" Hawkeye snapped, still seething. The group followed Chingachgook into the woods, soon picking up the trail the Wendats had left.

32
Rest
22:23

The canoes stopped on the shore of the lake, and Magua's men pulled the ladies onto the dry land. They walked for a few minutes to get off the beach before stopping in a small clearing of trees where Magua's men began to make a fire.

David and the ladies sat in a circle and discussed their situation in hushed whispers. Magua glanced over at them every couple of seconds, suspicious of what they were talking about.

"They've kept us alive this long, I do not believe that they intend to kill us," David said.

Cora nodded, stroking Alice's hand to calm her.

"What do you think they intend to do with us?" Alice asked.

"Magua wants to marry Cora, or at least keep her as some sort of slave. As for you, Miss Alice, I have not the faintest idea. He might want to sell you to the French, or he may ask for ransom himself. He even may decide to let you go, seeing as it is truly Cora he wants, but I cannot know what the man is thinking…" David trailed off.

"Should we try to escape?" Alice asked.

"No, we are too far north now; we are not near anything. We would die from exposure before we found a safe haven," Cora responded.

Alice nodded. "Then what do we do?"

"I would say we should pray that your father finds us," David said. "But," he began whispering. "…we must leave them a trail to follow."

"How do we do that? We have taken a canoe up the river. They will have no means of knowing where we went!" Cora hissed.

"Aye, but those attempting to find us would be smart enough to know that Magua is taking us to his village, or at least into Huron territory. If they know the general direction, they will eventually be able to find our trail, if we leave it heavy enough," David responded. "Magua and his men know how to leave no trail, and their moccasins are made to hide it. But we are wearing hard-soled shoes, and we may leave imprints deep enough to be tracked. We may break branches, leave bits of cloth, anything that would show our heroes which direction we have taken."

"Cora!" Magua's voice rang out. The girl lifted her head to make eye contact with the Wendat chief. "I desire your presence at my fire," he ordered, his lips curled up on one side. Cora opened her mouth to give him a verbal lashing, then she decided against it; there was no need to give him a reason to hurt Alice.

She rose and approached the man gingerly, lowering herself to the ground opposite him. However, he shook his head and motioned for her to sit beside him. She bit her lip and rolled her eyes before doing as he asked. He smirked, turning to face her.

"I would like to get to know you, Cora," he said.

How dare he?

The man had just kidnapped her and her sister from their father and now he wanted her to be civil with him.

"What does the Huron want to know?" she questioned, not giving him the satisfaction of hearing his name on her lips.

"As much as I can in our time on this trip, my dear. Let's start with the basics. Where are you from?"

She grimaced but did not comment on his idea. "Dunbar, Scotland."

"What is your favorite thing to do in the world?"

Cora paused for a second, actually considering the question. She had many things she enjoyed doing, but what gave her the most joy?

"I must say...dancing with my sister. Not the proper dances at the balls, just running around and being a fool," she said, smiling at the memories.

Magua nodded.

"And what is your greatest memory?"

"Oh, that is easy," she said. "Alice and I once discovered a field of flowers in the woods behind our manor. Running around like fools in a bed of sweet-smelling flowers... I will never forget the pure innocence and joy we had..." she trailed off.

"How old were you?"

"This was... three years ago, I believe. So I would have been seventeen, and Alice would have been almost fourteen."

"So you are twenty years of age?"

Cora nodded. "Yes. I turned twenty on the boat ride over here."

"What is your date of birth?"

"Fourteen July 1737," she replied. Her voice was still flat and uncaring, but she still asked in return, "When is yours?"

"I am unsure of the exact day, but it was twenty-six years past, sometime in the spring..."

"I see..." she said.

The man put a finger under her chin and turned her to look at him. Cora stiffened but stood her ground, not pulling away.

"You hate me now, my dear, but someday you will grow to love me," he said, giving what appeared to be a genuine smile.

Cora looked up at him, her brows furrowed. *Is he really just doing this for revenge on Father?*

11 August 1757

33
Separation

05:32

T he group woke up to the Wendats hauling them to their feet. Alice began shrieking, as their aggression frightened her. Magua was approaching them quickly. Cora took a step backward as he walked up to her.

"I must leave you now, my dear, but I will return to you," he promised. He picked up her hand and laid a gentle kiss on it. She pulled her hand out of his grasp.

"Where are you going?" she questioned.

"Where am I going? You mean, where are we going?" he said, his lips curling up into a smirk as he grabbed Alice by the wrist and pulled her away.

Alice began screaming again, calling out for her sister. One of Magua's men restrained Cora, who was trying to chase after her sister, begging Magua to let them remain together.

"David! Go with her! Please, in God's name, stay with her!" Cora cried out. David nodded, sprinting after the girl and the Wendat chief. Then Cora was dragged away herself, a warrior holding each of her arms.

Alice begged Magua to bring her back to her sister. "Please, sir, I will behave, I will not protest, I will slave away for your people my whole life, but do not keep me from her! Please!" she begged, tears pouring down her cheeks.

Magua ignored her pleas, yanking her along with him, some of his men following behind them.

"For God's sake, please!" she cried, digging her heels into the ground. He paused and turned to look at her.

"Enough, woman! There is reason behind everything I do, I assure you! I am not doing this to hurt you, or your sister! You will see her again, so stop whimpering in my ear!" he shouted.

Alice cringed at his raised voice but bit her lip and stopped resisting.

The walk wasn't long, no more than twenty minutes. Magua dragged Alice into the Huron camp and handed her off to Teharihoyen without a word, then walked into the longhouse to discuss the events at Fort William Henry with the sachem and sagamores of his tribe.

Teharihoyen released his tight grip on Alice's arm as he led her toward another longhouse on the edge of the village. She said nothing to him, small tears falling from the corners of her eyes as she walked.

He pushed open the door to the longhouse and led her inside. There was a woman lying on the ground, covered in a thick fur blanket. She was sweating profusely and her eyes were clenched shut as if she was in a lot of pain.

"You are to stay in here with her. I will not make you do anything, but she is sick and dying. Any comfort you can provide to her would be greatly appreciated," Teharihoyen said. Alice looked down at the woman and then back up to him. His eyes were trained on the woman, brow furrowed.

Alice nodded and picked up a cloth and bowl that sat beside the woman's head. She dipped the cloth in the water and wrung it out, laying the now-cool cloth on the woman's head.

Teharihoyen's lips twitched as he watched the young woman immediately jump into nursing the sick woman. He turned and exited the longhouse.

34
David

15:45

T he men sat hunched around the glowing coals of the campfire, discussing their prospects. The colonel had been almost inconsolable with grief all day, certain that his daughters were already dead. It took everything for Hawkeye to reassure him that Magua had no intention of killing them, especially Cora.

Uncas joined the group from the woods, taking a seat beside his brother. He had been out following the path Magua had taken Cora.

"It's a Delaware camp, the people of the Turtle," he said, his voice rising with excitement. The colonel's brow raised.

"How is that useful, my boy? The Delaware have sided with the French. Who are the Turtle people?"

"We are Mohicans. Mohicans and Turtles are cut from the same branch. We're all Delaware, but there are many Delaware. Mohicans and Turtles came from the same people," Uncas explained.

"You are like cousins, then?" the colonel asked.

"Cousins, brothers. My grandfather lived among the Turtle, before the fall," the young Mohican responded.

"I ken," Munro said. Uncas took his seat at the fire and began eating the bird his father had cooked for him while they awaited his arrival.

"I will go searching for Miss Alice as soon as I finish eating!" Uncas assured the old colonel. Munro nodded, giving a small smile of appreciation.

"Thank you, son." He groaned as he rose to his feet and crossed over to where Uncas had taken a seat. Uncas offered his shoulder to help Munro lower himself to the ground next to him.

"I am terribly sorry for how I treated you before, lad. I was raised to only respect people who are polished and proud... I thought, well I assumed those who do not share the same traditions as me must be savages, but I now realize this is not true. You and your family... Well you may not have the same manners and religion as them, but you have all the bravery and honor as the knights of the past. I... I understand this now, but it is hard for me to fight these innate biases against your people, and against you. But, I am trying..." Munro struggled through the apology, wanting to smack himself about the head as he realized what an arse he had been.

Uncas put a hand up to stop the colonel's rambles. "Colonel, I forgive you. There is no need to explain why you are how you are. Almost every man of your complexion has treated us the same... It is a foolish way of thinking."

Munro put a hand on Uncas' shoulder. "How can you be so forgiving? I was horrible to you, and not forty hours ago. I do not understand how you can have grace..."

"Miss Cora once told me everyone deserves grace, even Magua. She said your God offers forgiveness to all who ask. Why then should I be unforgiving?" Uncas replied.

"And my daughter... You care about her?" Munro asked, recognizing the emotions in the man's voice.

"Your daughter...I have never met a woman like her, sir. You may believe yourself to have been raised with prejudices and hatred, but you have raised your daughter without any. She is kind and open-minded— a brilliant woman," Uncas said, a smile gracing his lips.

"I thank you; she is just like her mother..." Munro smiled, thinking about his fallen wife. "Will we find my daughter? Will we truly reach her before that villain harms her?" he asked, his voice filling with emotion.

"Sir, Magua will not hurt her, at least not physically. We just need to find some way to reach her and her sister without alerting the Huron. We are too few to take on his village alone, but with his village and the Turtle, we would never survive."

"I see, so we must discover where my Alice is?"

"Yes, Colonel."

Just as Uncas replied to the colonel, the group heard a rustling in the trees to their right. They all shot to their feet, hands gripping their hatchets and knives.

"It's just me!" David's voice rang out before they saw him. He rushed into the clearing, approaching the men with a grin on his face. "I knew you men would come! Have you found Miss Cora?"

"Yes, Uncas tracked her to a Delaware village some fifteen minutes east of here," Chingachgook replied.

"Wonderful, and I have brought news of Miss Alice!"

"You have? Where is she, sir? Where?!" Munro demanded, taking steps toward the psalmodist.

"In a Huron village, Magua's village. It is twenty minutes west of here. The girl is being kept in a longhouse on the edge of the village; she is tending to a sick woman. Magua is, I believe, going to the nearby Delaware village right now to go talk with Cora. I do not think he cares to check on the youngest Miss Munro until he has ensured that we are not going to save Cora. So we should retrieve Alice first, and then once

Magua has returned to the Huron village, we should go to rescue Cora and make our escape," David said in a rush.

"You are truly brilliant, David!" Hawkeye said, grabbing the man's arm and shaking him with excitement. "This may yet work."

35
Reed that Bends
16:57

H eyward trailed behind Uncas, trying to stay silent. His army-issued black boots, made to march in pretty lines, were not particularly quiet. But Uncas' soft skin moccasins were almost undetectable in the forest. Heyward felt like he was giving them away. The night was dark, but not quiet, and the locusts sang, but even so, Heyward's boots were loud.

Something rustled ahead of them, and Uncas crouched instantly, pulling Heyward down with him. A man, nay a boy, came into view. He looked around skittishly, his eyes darting about the woods. Heyward could see him shaking.

The boy was a Wendat and couldn't have been more than sixteen, with the Mohawk that Heyward had seen on many of the warriors at the massacre. He held the side of the musket barrel, instead of the bottom, next to his hip and away from his body. He looked as if he had never held a gun in his life. Heyward noted that the hatchet at his waist also appeared pristine, and sharp, without a drop of blood on it.

He got closer and closer to the two men, clearly oblivious to their presence. Uncas had a hand on Heyward's shoulder, keeping him still. Heyward's heart was thumping, as the boy was no more than two meters away from them.

Heyward kept himself low and rested his arms on his knees, but when his weight switched, a small twig under his boot snapped. The young Wendat turned and wildly fired his musket in a panic. He missed the men by meters, but he made eye contact with Heyward and his eyes got big. Turning, he sprinted away. Uncas leapt to his feet and chased the boy to stop him from rousing the other men.

Heyward rose, realizing he couldn't sprint through the woods without causing a ruckus, and stared in the dark at Uncas' retreating form. Both Uncas and the young Wendat soon disappeared, and Heyward continued standing there, completely unaware of his surroundings.

He stayed like that for quite a while before he realized something must have happened. Uncas would have certainly caught the boy before now. If he had not returned yet, something must have happened to him. Heyward began running in the direction Uncas had gone, no longer concerned if someone heard him. If Uncas had been hurt, he might not have time to waste.

As Heyward raced into a clearing, he saw Uncas standing between two very large Wendat warriors. A third warrior held the boy by the arms. Then two other men appeared behind Heyward before he could even process what had happened, and then both he and Uncas were frog-marched toward what he presumed was the Huron camp.

36
Miss Munro's Malice

18:00

C ora was sitting on the bed in the corner of the wigwam when the blanket covering the door swung open. Magua stood in the threshold. He was grinning at her.

"You are mine now."

"That is not true! I will never marry you," she protested, standing to argue with the offensive man.

"You already have. You are here, in my home. I have taken you to wife."

"No marriages done without God are valid. You forget my faith, villain." She practically spat the words at him.

Magua tilted his head. "If that is what you wish, I can have the singer brought in. I am sure he would agree to do the ceremony with a knife at his throat. All men say they do not fear death, but when it stares them in the face, they always piss themselves."

Cora swallowed, watching him carefully.

"Leave David out of this. If you say we are married, there is nothing I can truly do about it, but even so, I cannot understand your reasons."

She approached him and stood right in front of him, arms crossed. "You have said it is to get revenge on the gray-haired colonel, and yet during your comrades' vicious attack, you never even attacked my father, caring so little that you left him to your men. How could he appreciate your revenge if they killed him?"

"You are too smart for your own good, Cora," he said, smirking as he looked her up and down.

"Do not call me Cora. You have no right!"

"And what kind of husband does not call his wife by her given name?" He chuckled at the joke. "There is truth in your words, Cora. I was not paying attention to the Yengee chief. My whole vision has been clouded."

She shivered as his dark eyes trailed down her neck, across her whole body, and then back up to her face. "You are a very intriguing woman, and I find myself admiring you more and more each day."

She recoiled, her nose crinkling with disgust. "How dare you, you evil fox! This is no plan to revenge yourself on my father. It is your own perversion that fuels it! I could have stomached marrying you for my family's sake, but I will not be your war trophy, brought here for you to lust after!"

Magua's face remained calm, almost as if he had been expecting such a response.

Tears flowed freely. "And then this…" Cora motioned to herself and to him. "…this shall not be some prison in which I slave away for you. Will you force yourself on me? Such an act would degrade me, so that I could not bear to continue living, I swear it!"

His lips drew out into a thin line. "Calm yourself. I have no intention of forcing you to do anything, Cora. You will grow to love me."

Cora wiped the tears away from her eyes.

"And my innocent sister? What will you do when Alice grows weary and ill? She cannot take this life of mine well or survive in this world without me. She will throw herself from a cliff. My sister's pain will be your fault. She has done nothing to you, and yet you would see her dead!"

"The light hair will be safe. I have no intention of hurting her. She will live her days in peace with my people, so long as she does nothing foolish."

"And what of my men? What of Uncas, who will surely come for me? What of my father, who is no doubt on my trail? And what of Hawkeye, the only man you fear, devil?" Cora poked a finger into his chest.

Magua raised a hand to slap her, and she flinched away, anticipating the blow, but his hand retracted and he grimaced. He turned and without a word, left her in the wigwam, alone, save the guards posted at her door.

37
Captured

18:13

Two Wendats led Heyward away from the middle of the village the second they got there. He could tell that he meant nothing to them; they only cared about the young Mohican they had captured.

The men holding Heyward brought him to a longhouse on the edge of the village; there were two women standing outside, guarding the building. The men said something to the ladies in Wyandot and opened the door to the longhouse, pushing Heyward inside.

Alice was sitting on the ground next to a native woman lying under a fur blanket. It was mid-August and had to be at least 70°; the woman was sick. She was pale, too pale, and sweat dripped down her face.

Alice was clad in a buckskin dress and the same moccasins that the Mohicans and Hawkeye always wore. Her hair was flowing free down her back, with no intricate designs or braids.

The British officer held a finger to his lips to ensure she said nothing to him until they knew it was safe. One of the men who had brought him there remained as his guard, while the other left.

"Are you alright, Alice?" Heyward questioned, barely above a whisper. His eyebrows furrowed as he put a hand on her shoulder.

She nodded and gave him a weak smile.

"They did not hurt me, just put me in here, with her. I do not know what is wrong with her or if it is catching; being in here with her might very well be a death sentence," she explained. Heyward nodded, and the two discussed everything that had happened.

Uncas was brought to the center of the village with the young brave he had chased in the forest earlier. His captors ignored him at first, focusing on the young Wendat.

"Tehora~ati,[1] I have been told that you, once again, have run from battle," the Wendat chief said in Wyandot. The man was beautifully dressed with long white and blue feathers tied among his braids. "I have been told that you ran into this Delaware in the woods, and after missing your shot at him, you turned and ran," the sachem said, his face a mask with no emotion.

"The Manitoo[2] has made you pleasing to the eye but it would be better if you had not been born. None of my young warriors strike the tomahawk so deeply into the war post-none of them so lightly on the Yengees. Three times you have been called on to fight, and three times you have not given an answer. The enemy knows the shape of your back, but they have never seen the color of your eyes. Now let your

---

1. The name Tehora~ati means "He runs, escapes from them" in Wyandot.

2. The Manitoo is the head spiritual deity of many Northeastern tribes. Generally, it is spelled Manitou. However, I have retained Cooper's original spelling of Manitoo.

name never again be spoken in your tribe. It is already forgotten," he finished, motioning toward an older man standing off to the side.

The man came forward, stone-faced as he stared at the younger man. The boy looked upon the man, trembling. Uncas did not speak the Wendat language, but when the boy looked up at the man, tears in his eyes, and uttered "ha'isten," Uncas understood the relationship.

The man was his father. The young boy was looking at his father with pleading eyes, clearly desperate to be accepted by the man. However, it was not to be, because the father could not stand to look at his son. The boy he had raised had turned out to be a coward.

Uncas watched, his face stone cold while his heart sank for the poor boy, as the father unsheathed a large knife. The boy took a step back and began pleading aloud with the man. He fell to his knees and grabbed his father's legs, crying against them, begging for his life.

The father buried his knife in the boy's chest and the pleas that had torn at Uncas' heart were silenced. Once the boy had fallen to the ground, everyone began turning on Uncas. He squared his shoulders, standing between two large warriors, who could grab him at any moment.

Without hesitating, the young Mohican broke off into a sprint. The guards behind him tried to grab his arms, but he slipped right through them and escaped their grasp. He almost made it to the edge of the camp before a few warriors cut him off. He turned and sprinted in another direction, but the men there raised their knives at him. His eyes widened as he realized he couldn't escape via that path either.

He tried again and again, the men getting closer and closer to him on all sides. Realizing he had no hope of escaping at that moment, Uncas threw himself on the pole of one of the longhouses. The men all pulled up short, their faces falling.

"He has claimed his right of protection!" the sachem announced. "Bring him into the longhouse, and we will discuss what to do with him when *Le Renard Subtil* returns." Three men then approached Uncas and he fought the urge to fight them or attempt to flee again as they dragged him off to the longhouse to be tied up before the sagamores.

38
Magua's Return

21:08

U ncas' wrists were starting to chafe from the rope binding them together, but the young Mohican could barely feel the pain. Instead, his head swarmed with thoughts of escape. If he was a captive, who would save Cora?

The door to the longhouse was flung open and Uncas heard footsteps. The sachem began conversing with the man in Wyandot. Uncas only picked up every couple of words, but he heard one clear as glass: Magua.

Magua greeted the sachem, who invited him to sit so that they might discuss what had happened in the village since Magua left.

"There have been strangers around our village as of late; one of them has been caught. We found him chasing one of our young warriors, who we have disposed of and forgotten."

Magua nodded, already knowing which warrior it must have been; Tehora~ati had been running from battle since he was first told to fight.

"And did my young men kill the stranger?"

The sachem didn't say a word; he only tilted his head toward Uncas in the corner. Magua turned his head lazily to see the intruder but froze when he caught sight of the young Mohican. He leapt to his feet and began walking toward Uncas, looking him up and down, unsure if this dream of his was coming true.

"*Le Cerf Agile!*" Magua shouted, drawing his knife and pointing it at Uncas. Those gathered in the longhouse began arguing about Magua's accusation. The noise became more and more raucous until the sachem raised his hand for silence.

Magua began retelling the story of what had happened at Glen, all in English, so the Mohican understood his speech. The men who didn't understand English crowded around a young warrior who repeated what he said in Wyandot.

"*Le Cerf Agile* was among those that fought at Glen. He is in league with *Le Gros Serpent* and *La Longue Carabine*. Forty Wendat warriors died that day," Magua said, looking around and making eye contact with his tribesman. "Are the bones of my young men in the burial place of the Huron? You know they are not. Their spirits have gone toward the setting sun, and are already crossing the great waters to the happy hunting grounds," he said with animation.

He crouched beside the sachem and sagamores and addressed them all personally. "But they departed without food, without guns or knives, without moccasins— naked and poor as they were born!" He stood and addressed the crowd, "Shall this be? Are their souls to enter the land of the just hungry and bare, or shall they meet their friends there with arms in their hands and robes on their backs?"

Magua stood, grabbing the wrist of one of the women who circled the crowd. "What will our fathers think the tribes of the Wyandots have become?" He looked at her with wild eyes and released her, dropping her wrist. He stood and returned to the center of the crowd. "Brothers, we must not forget the Huron dead!" He took a few steps toward Uncas and grabbed him by his chin. "We will load the back of this Mohican until he staggers under our bounty, then we will dispatch him after my young men." He took a step away from Uncas and addressed the crowd again, "They call to us for aid. They cry 'Forget us not!'"

As Magua's voice rose with each syllable Uncas saw firsthand the leadership qualities in this Wendat that had convinced two scores of his brethren to follow him to their deaths. "When they see the spirit of this Mohican toiling after them with his burden, they will know we did not forget them, and they will go on happy! Let this Mohican die!" Magua shouted, again pointing his knife at Uncas' chest. The crowd erupted into cheers, their blood lust encouraged by Magua's rousing speech.

Magua silenced them all with a single hand gesture, making eye contact with Uncas.

Realizing that the Wendat expected a response, Uncas raised his chin, his eyes shining.

"The healing waters will never bring the dead Hurons to life. The tumbling river washes their bones; their men are women, their women owls. I smell the blood of a coward. Go! Call together your Huron dogs, that they might look upon a warrior. Show them how a Mohican can die!"

39
Magua's Plan
22:25

U ncas stood tall against the pole, his shoulders rising and falling with every breath. The longhouse was empty. The chiefs and sachem with him earlier had left. It was getting late, and Uncas supposed all the warriors had long since sought their beds. He was all alone with his thoughts. How could a man fall asleep when he was to die in only a few hours?

The door to the longhouse opened and Magua stepped inside. Uncas straightened his back, standing tall. Why was the Wendat chief here?

"You are going to die tomorrow, Mohican. How will your father feel, being the last of his kind?"

"We have been the last for a decade now, dog. My father is at peace with this," Uncas said, trying to keep the spite from his lips. His father would expect him to be brave in the face of death, and that he should be ready to die, but Uncas was frightened. He did not want to die, not while the eldest Miss Munro was in peril. He might not be able to make a life with such a woman, but she was perfection, and perfection should be cherished and protected.

"You may think so, but I know how to torture my enemies beyond the grave. You will never be at peace, nor will your father." Magua gave him a look of such hatred, his eyes piercing Uncas' own, something that surprised the Mohican. Magua had always been an enemy. They had fought on opposite sides of the war, but Uncas had never hated him until the situation with Cora.

Magua leaned against the wall, silently observing Uncas. He was contemplating something, but Uncas couldn't fathom what that was.

"The white men have taken over the Earth," Magua began.

"This is true," Uncas agreed.

"They are plaguing everyone, and the only way for us to continue as we were before is to get rid of all of them," Magua said, pushing himself away from the wall and walking toward Uncas. "They are evil and must be destroyed. How can you support them? They wiped your tribe from the Earth!"

Uncas shifted from foot to foot. He knew that in some ways, Magua was right. The white men had only been there a few hundred years, and they had already gained complete control over any nearby tribes. They also seemed insatiable, determined to drive the natives from the land, but Uncas couldn't bring himself to hate them, or even countenance the idea of killing them. They were not all a cursed people; just the ones in control seemed hellbent on pushing his people to extinction.

"They are thirsty for our land. Only a fool would be blind to that. But I do not believe that killing them is the solution. We stop them, and why kill so many, many of which are innocent?" Uncas countered.

"Innocent?" Magua shouted at him. "How can you say any of them are innocent? Even their children spit on us. I was in a fort, Mohican... I know, I saw how they treated our kind; they all despise us, so they should all die!" Magua paused, considering something. "I would let you go if you helped me, Mohican. I need an army, and you can help me. Your father, too. All I would request is the death of La Longue Carabine."

Uncas shook his head. "You think there is anything that could compel me to turn over my brother to you?!"

"He is not your brother. His people are responsible for the death of your tribe, Mohican!"

"You speak of Hawkeye as if his whole race is a menace. There are some good among them! You cannot disagree with that," Uncas spat back.

"There are none."

"And Cora?" Uncas challenged.

Magua's eyes narrowed.

"How can you justify taking her to wife while killing all her people? How can you call them all evil and worthy of death, but do everything in your power to kidnap and keep her?"

"You seem to care a great deal about the lady..." Magua said, raising an eyebrow at Uncas.

"She does not deserve your wrath and you know it. You are keeping her for your own selfish desires, but you will never deserve her," Uncas replied bitterly.

Magua smirked. "You love her," he said, taking another step toward Uncas.

Uncas blanched. Magua's knowledge of his feelings for Miss Munro would do nothing but endanger both of them.

"It does not take loving someone to see they deserve better than a dirty fox." Uncas' lip curled.

"You love her," Magua said with a nod. "And because of your love for her, I must inform you that the lady of your affections is unavailable. Cora Munro is already married." Magua's lips pulled into a wide grin.

"No, she's not!" Uncas shouted. "You taking her does not make her yours! She will never return your affections, not for a hundred years!"

"I have already had her, Mohican," Magua lied.

Uncas started pulling against the pole, doing everything he could to get free and kill the villain.

"I'll kill you, you monster!" Magua leaned his head back, laughing. He took a step back and turned to leave.

"You will die tomorrow, Mohican. And it will be slow. And do not worry about the woman; she will forget about you when she warms my bed," he said as he closed the door behind him.

Now alone, Uncas kept pulling against the pole, desperate to free himself and kill the evil man.

12 August 1757

40
Escape
01:43

Alice held the cold compress to the woman's forehead. Duncan had helped to remove the blanket and place several other wet pieces of cloth elsewhere on the Huron woman's body. This seemed to cool her down a little, but she was still flushed and covered in a light sheen of sweat.

After a few hours in the longhouse, David returned to them. He told them he had been to see the men in the forest, and they had discussed what they were going to do, especially now that Uncas was a captive.

"What are we going to do, Duncan?" Alice asked, looking around the longhouse. "The men are surely going to be focused on rescuing Uncas because Magua wants to kill him tomorrow. But we need to escape tonight or Magua will realize what is happening and could kill us to cut his losses," she said, almost shaking.

"I think we're going to have to get out of here on our own..." Duncan said.

David nodded. "I believe you're correct, Major."

As they were discussing this, the door to the longhouse opened and Teharihoyen walked in, eyeing the three suspiciously.

"How is she?" he asked.

Alice looked up at him, her brow furrowing. She stood and approached the man slowly.

"Teharihoyen, she can still live," Alice said. "She was doing so poorly before because her fever was burning through her like fire. We've cooled her down, but she is still too hot. If we were to submerge her in cool water—"

"You want me to let you take her out into the woods? You are using my wife's illness to escape!" Teharihoyen accused, pointing a finger at the young woman.

Alice sucked in a breath as she realized the relationship between the two of them.

She shook her head. "No, Teharihoyen. You are the only person in this village who has been kind to me; I would never betray you like that. But I do believe bringing down her temperature is the only way to save her."

The man frowned at her, then finally nodded.

"Very well, help me carry her, sir," Teharihoyen said to Heyward, crouching down beside his wife and gently slipping his hand underneath her shoulders. Heyward nodded, grabbed the woman's ankles, and helped the Huron lift her up. She groaned, and Teharihoyen's eyes got big as he tried to lower her back down, but Alice convinced him that it was alright; it was just a short walk to the lake.

They exited the longhouse and Teharihoyen said something in Wendat to the guard, which Alice presumed was an explanation of where they were going. The man frowned, but after one look at Teharihoyen's wife, and he stepped out of their way.

They carried the woman into the woods toward the lake that the village used for water. The Huron people had carved out an inlet for the river water to flow into, so that they could have fresh water that was safe for the children to be around.

The group approached the water and walked waist-deep into it, carrying the woman in as well. She gasped as her body came into contact with the water and then she began grasping frantically at Teharihoyen. He leaned in close to her and whispered something in her ear.

"Keep her in the water; it will lower her body temperature, and she may beat the fever," Alice said with a gentle hand on the woman's shoulder to calm her down.

The woman muttered incoherently and groaned every couple of seconds, but soon, her body actually began to cool down. Alice could hear Teharihoyen's sobs, and she took a step toward him.

"She will live, Teharihoyen. Why are you crying?"

"I thought there was n-no hope for her. I have spent the p-past week trying to help our daughter understand that she was going to lose her m-mother. Dear girl, I am so incredibly grateful for your efforts," he said, putting his hands over his face as he shook with emotion.

Alice watched as the pent-up fear of losing his wife was released in another torrent of tears.

"Teharihoyen,[1] you are an amazing husband. You and your family will live many happy years together," Alice said, giving the man a genuine smile. He looked at his wife for a brief second before turning his head back to Alice.

"Leave! Get as far from here as you can. I will come up with some story of how you got away, but you need to go, now!" he said sharply.

Alice smiled, planting a kiss on her hand and pressing it to the woman's forehead before running after Duncan and David into the

---

1. The name Teharihoyen means "He is a matter divided in two" in Wyandot.

forest. Alice found it was much easier to move fast in the buckskin dress she had been given than the heavy petticoats of her gowns. She caught up with the men and then the three kept running for nearly ten minutes before they reached the clearing.

The three of them burst into the clearing. At first, it appeared empty, Hawkeye and Chingachgook still off rescuing Uncas. However, one of the bushes on the edge of the clearing rustled, and Heyward stepped in front of Alice, eyeing it with concern. Suddenly, the colonel popped his head up and broke into a grin when he saw them.

"Papa!" Alice cried, rushing to her father. She helped him to his feet and wrapped him in a tight hug.

"My dear, I canna believe you're safe. I thought I'd lost you." He kissed her temple and held her head to his chest as they embraced.

"I'm here Papa, and I'm alright. They didn't hurt me."

"God be praised," Munro said as he kissed her forehead.

"Amen," the psalmodist said with a smile.

Uncas' face was still red with anger. He was just waiting for the opportunity to free himself and kill the villain for what he had done to Cora.

Suddenly, his head snapped to the side at the sound of a knife digging into the wood at the back of the longhouse. Someone was trying to break inside, and there were only a few people with the ability and motivation to do that.

Sliding through the small hole that he and Hawkeye had created, Chingachgook silently cut the ropes that bound Uncas' hands behind the pole. Uncas laid a hand on his heart, nodding to his father as he stepped away from the pole, rubbing the chafe marks on his wrists.

Chingachgook gave a knife to Uncas, who put his back up against the pole and his arms behind it to feign still being tied there. Seconds later, Hawkeye appeared through the hole and the men all nodded to each other before the scout and his father hid.

The longhouse was an L shape. Uncas was in the middle of the long side, while the sagamores' seats on the rug were at the bottom of the long side opposite the entrance. Chingachgook and Hawkeye hid in the small section of the room that formed the short side of the L.

Uncas began yelling some French phrases he had picked up fighting the Wendats. "The Hurons are pathetic, crying women. They all run when faced with real men! They are all like Tehora~ati!"

The Wendats guarding the door to the longhouse both entered red-faced, their eyes gleaming with hatred. Uncas smirked at them as they approached.

One of them snarled, "Magua has said you are to die tomorrow, but he didn't say we couldn't hurt you, Mohican dog."

The man on the right raised his fist to plant a facer, but then froze and toppled over as Chingachgook's knife thrust into his back. The old Mohican snapped a hand around the man's mouth and lowered him to the ground.

Hawkeye wrapped his hand around the other man's mouth and Uncas pulled away from the pole, digging his knife into the Wendat's stomach. He twisted it and pulled it up, spilling the man's guts. The two brothers scalped their victims and turned to their father.

Chingachgook lingered in the small section of the room, away from the door, observing a bear pelt that was lying there. The brothers joined their father.

A little boy entered the longhouse. He gaped when he saw the bodies of the guards on the ground. He could not see the men, but they knew he was there.

Hawkeye wrapped the cloak around his body and got down on his hands and knees. He crawled out in front of the little boy, pretending not to see the child. White-faced, the little boy slapped a hand over his mouth and slowly backed toward the exit. Once he had gone, the three men instantly exited the longhouse and sprinted into the woods, praying that the child's confusion would give them enough time to escape.

41
Sanctuary
02:27

Chingachgook, Hawkeye, and Uncas burst into the clearing where Alice, Duncan, David, and Colonel Munro were waiting. They could not hear anyone behind them yet, but they knew it could not be long before the Wendats were on their trail.

"A child saw me," Hawkeye said in a rush. "He will surely tell his parents about the bear, and they will find Uncas missing. We must away!"

Alice raised an eyebrow.

"The bear?"

"I will explain everything later, but we must go..."

"To the Delaware village!" Chingachgook said. "Delaware do not turn away strangers; as long as we are not threatening, they will give us sanctuary!"

"This means we will have to stash our weapons and be unarmed," Uncas said.

"Yes, but at least we will be alive," his father countered.

Uncas nodded, and the group turned toward the lake. Uncas approached the colonel.

"There's no time to lose, sir," he said, turning his back to the colonel and bending down to one knee. The colonel nodded and climbed atop the Mohican's back. The group took off running. Alice, however, soon lagged behind. Realizing she was trailing behind, Hawkeye ran back to her, collecting her in his arms like she weighed nothing, and running after his family.

Her heart thumped in her chest as she wrapped her arms around his shoulders. *How can he carry me and still run so fast?* He was a large man with impossibly broad shoulders; if any man was up to the task, it was him.

The group reached the edge of the lake and all piled into two canoes. They pushed away from the shore and out onto the lake, the light of the moon shining down on them. The men paddled smoothly, each stroke deep into the water, propelling them forward. They were somehow all perfectly in sync; it was as if they had practiced this their whole lives.

Alice ran her fingers through her long golden hair, trying to detangle it as it had gotten a lot of knots in it during the race to the clearing with Duncan and David. Once her hair met her standard, she used the knife Chingachgook had given her to cut a small string of leather from the sleeve of her buckskin dress. Then she reached her hands behind her head and began braiding her hair. She was conscious that Hawkeye was sitting close behind her, so she was careful not to whip him in the face when she brought her hair around the front to finish and tie the end of her braid with her little bit of leather. Her hands skimmed the edge of her hair, checking for bumps and flyaways, but she was satisfied with her work. When she had finished, she turned to look at the man behind her.

"Well, Hawkeye, will you tell me what bear you were referring to?" she asked him playfully. He smirked at her question.

"Of course, my lady. When my father and I went to retrieve Uncas a young Huron saw the dead guards, so I used the bear cloak that was sitting in the corner of the room and scared him away. Of course, the little boy was sure to run to his parents and tell them of the bear, but they would know there was no such animal," Hawkeye explained.

Alice laughed heartily. "My, that is clever! Of course, such a trick would not work for most people; it takes an enormous man to convincingly play a bear!" she said, chuckling and turning back to look ahead.

"An enormous man, aye?" he questioned, his grin lopsided. "Tell me, dear Alice..." He leaned in behind her and whispered into her ear, his voice deep and rough. "Would you think me a bear?" The girl's words caught in her throat as her cheeks turned red.

"Oh, I...um, I am certain I would be able to recognize you in a bear pelt... Yes, I certainly would!" she protested, unable to hold back her grin.

"Hmm, maybe you would..." he said, laughing.

The group soon reached the edge of the lake and exited the canoes. Chingachgook carried the men's rifles into the woods to hide them while the rest of the group approached the village. As they got closer, they saw the Delawares watching them. No one moved in their direction but several men were brandishing their knives.

Uncas went up to one of them and told him they were unarmed and seeking sanctuary. The man nodded and began leading them toward a wigwam. When they reached the entrance, the man pulled aside a blanket that covered it.

"Uncas?" Cora questioned, seeing the man. His eyes got big, and the group rushed into the wigwam to greet her. She threw her arms around Alice and her father.

"My dear, are you alright?" Munro asked, his arms still wrapped around Cora's frame.

"I am; Magua has not hurt me. But, he says that I am his woman, that he took me, so I am his," she said through heavy breaths. "Is that true?"

"The rules around marriage are not exact, my dear. Anyone can claim they are married if they both say so," Chingachgook responded, entering the wigwam.

"So I am not married?" she asked in a hopeful voice.

"It does not matter what he says, dear sister. You answer to God, and God alone," Alice replied. Cora nodded, accepting this answer.

"Cora!" Uncas said, pulling her toward him. She was a bit shocked at the forward gesture but leaned into his body as he held her close. "The devil told me he had...taken liberties with you... that you had laid with him," Uncas whispered into her ear.

Sucking in a breath, Cora shook her head. "He has not, Uncas. Do not fear." She put a hand over his heart, where she could feel it beating rapidly. She leaned her head against his chest and put her arms over his shoulders, behind his neck.

Uncas smiled as he wrapped his arms around her. He looked up over her shoulder to see Colonel Munro watching them. He pulled Cora away from him gently and leaned into her ear, bringing her attention to her father. She nodded and turned to address her father.

"Papa, I think we need to discuss the... elephant in the room," she said. He looked at her and nodded.

"Very well, what will you say to me, dear child?"

"Uncas, the Mohicans, are friends to me and Alice. I love you, Papa, but you have to accept this. I will not cut Uncas...the Mohicans out of my life on your orders, so you have to accept this," she said firmly. Munro bit his lip but eventually nodded.

"My dear, I have never accepted savage heathens, never... However, these heathens...these men have done everything in their power to bring you home safely to me, and it has made me realize they are not savages, not at all. I... Well, I will accept them into our lives. And I would be remiss as a father if I did not throw myself at their feet to beg forgiveness for how I have treated them," Munro said.

Heyward's eyes bugged, and he crossed his arms, taking a step back.

The three men inclined their heads, accepting his apology. Cora could see Hawkeye restraining himself from commenting, while his father and brother accepted the apology with grace. Alice and Cora both looked at their father with grins and threw their arms around him, proud of the aged man.

"He that covereth his sins shall not prosper: but whoso confesseth and forsaketh them shall have mercy," David said, smiling.

"Nulelìntàm èli paàn![1] " A voice rang out from outside in the clearing between the wigwams. It was Tessouat,[2] one of the sagamores of the village. There was barely a pause before the welcoming phrase was answered.

---

1. "Welcome" in Lenape.

2. The name Tessouat is of Algonquin origin; the meaning is unknown. It was the name of several Algonquin chiefs in the 17th century.

"Hè![3]" Magua called out the greeting. The group all turned at the sound of their enemy's voice. Not only was it concerning that Magua had gotten here so quickly, but as the man began speaking with Tessouat, it became clear that he had an excellent understanding of the Lenape tongue and a good relationship with the people as well.

---

3. Informal greeting in Lenape.

42

Tamenund

06:26

The group huddled at the back of the Delaware wigwam, watching from behind the hanging blanket that obscured them. Uncas translated what was happening in the center of the village for those in the group who did not understand Lenape. Magua sat in front of Tessouat. The man had long white and black feathers decorating his hair and black paint covering the bottom half of his face.

"The face of our Canada father turned against your Hurons?" The Delaware chief questioned Magua, who laughed.

"How could Tessouat ever believe such lies? He calls my people most beloved," said the Wendat.

Tessouat's eyes narrowed. "The tomahawks of your young men have been very red!" he argued, nodding at the scalps that hung from Magua's belt.

"It is so! But now they are bright and dull. The Yengees at Henry are dead, but there are others..." Magua trailed off. "Does my prisoner give trouble to my brother?"

Tessouat shook his head, glancing at the blanket that hid Cora from the sight of the Wendat. "No, she is welcome."

"The path between our villages is short. Let her be sent to my women if she gives trouble to my brother!" Magua said, making a grand waving gesture toward Tessouat as if to prove his good faith.

"She is welcome!" Tessouat insisted. Magua nodded, the corners of his lips twitching upward.

"Do my young men leave room enough on the mountains for the hunts of the Delaware?" he asked.

Tessouat's head rose at this question, his chin jutting out with pride.

"The Delawares are masters of their own hunting grounds!" Magua could sense that his Delaware friend was unhappy with him, and that wouldn't do if he was to retrieve Cora.

"It is well. The Delawares are loved by the Wendats! It pleases me that your men are doing so well!" Magua began acting the diplomat for the men in the wigwam, garnering sympathy. "Why should the Indians brighten their tomahawks against each other? The white men are thicker than the swallows in the seasons of the flowers!" This comment earned many approving shouts from those in the area.

Behind the curtain, Uncas translated this all, and Hawkeye cursed under his breath.

"Magua has always been good at convincing crowds to follow him. We'll need the support of the village to get out of here safely," Hawkeye muttered to his brother.

The conversation continued outside. "Have there not been strange moccasins in the woods?" Magua asked.

Tessouat's lips drew into a thin line.

"The French? Let the Canada father come; we are ready to see him!" he answered evasively.

Magua's head tilted to the side, a small frown on his face.

"The Canada father is welcome in the homes of the Wendat as well, but I speak not of him. The Yengees have long arms and legs that never tire, and my young men have dreamed that the Yengees walked into the village of the Delaware." Magua's voice was light, testing.

"They will not find the Delaware asleep," Tessouat spat, his voice rising.

Magua's eyes flashed.

"It is well, the warrior that leaves one eye open can always see his enemy." He retracted his attack and began reaching into the satchel that he had brought with him. "I have brought gifts for my brothers, the Delawares," Magua said, pulling out some of his spoils from the massacre.

"What is he pulling out, Uncas?" Cora asked.

"Loot. It looks like he got the best prizes from his men: a bribe."

Magua pulled out a pistol with "Bravery" engraved on the handle and one of the golden gorgets that had previously decorated the chest of some unfortunate English officer.

Sliding them across the ground to the chief, Magua gave what looked like a rehearsed smile. Tessouat stared at the gifts and the seemingly genuine face of the Wendat chief and cracks began to appear in his demeanor. Beads of sweat formed on his temples.

"Magua is a great chief; he is welcome..." Tessouat murmured.

Magua smiled. "The Wendats love their brothers the Delawares, and why should they not? They reside under the same sun, and they will go to the same hunting grounds after death. Red men should be friends!"

"There have been strange moccasins in our camp. We have tracked them into our lodges," Tessouat finally said.

"And did you beat out the dogs?" Magua questioned.

"It would not do; the stranger is always welcome in the homes of the Delaware!" Tessouat argued, lifting his chin

"The stranger, but not the spy," Magua countered.

Tessouat scoffed. "Would the Yengees send their women as spies? Did you not take women from the battle at Henry?" he demanded.

"So I did, and the Yengees sent their scouts and spies to chase after me. They went first to my village, you must know, Tessouat, but when they found no welcoming arms there, they approached your people, who they knew had turned from our Canada father!"

Tessouat rose to his feet with a shout. "Let the Canada father look me in the face! He will see no change! It is true my men did not fight with him against the Yengees on the lake, for we had dreams that said do not go. But we love and venerate our Canada father, Montcalm!"

"Will he think that when he hears that his enemy is fed in the camp of his children? Will he believe your loyalty when he learns that the Yengee who has slain so many of his young men, who is feared in the camps of the Delaware and Huron, has received refuge in your camp?" Magua countered, also rising.

"Who is this Yengee? Who is feared in my camp that I give refuge to?" Tessouat demanded.

"Count your prisoners, my brother. You will find among them a man whose skin is neither red nor white," Magua said.

Tessouat's eyebrow rose. "Who?"

"*La Longue Carabine*," Magua added. Shouts went up among those listening to the conversation. Tessouat's face turned cold and impassive. He turned to his deputy and gave him a quick order to bring out the sachem, Tamenund.[1]

The group watched from behind the blanket, as a decrepit, old man was led out from a large wigwam into the area where the encounter was taking place. He wore fine robes of carefully sewn hide with a richly beaded hem. There were beads sewn into patterns on his cloak as well—all turtles of some kind, and he wore a large wampum belt that also depicted turtles. The old man had long gray hair that was tied into two braids, fastened with large turquoise ornaments on the sides. His face was so wrinkled that his eyes could barely be seen amidst the folds.

"Bring them forward," the sachem demanded. A woman stood beside the blanket and pulled it open, beckoning the group into the center. The old sachem sat at the front of them, flanked by the sagamores Magua had talked to when he brought Cora to the village.

The group huddled together, wary of the unknown men and women around them. *Le Renard* stood before the sachem, talking in whispers to him. It was clear that the Wendat and the sachem were intimately acquainted.

For the first time, the sachem seemed to notice the Yengees and Mohicans. He beckoned them forward, to stand before him. Hawkeye,

---

1. James Fenimore Cooper based Tamenund on the great chief Tamenund of the Lenape, who signed the Shackamaxon Treaty with William Penn. However, the historical figure died around fifty years before the events of the book.

generally the confident one, held back, stooping to hide himself in the middle of the pack—an impossible task given his height.

"Come forward!" the old sachem commanded. "Who among you is *La Longue Carabine*?" None of the prisoners uttered a word. After a few seconds, Heyward stepped forward.

"I am *La Longue Carabine.*"

"This man is who we have heard so much about?" Tamenund questioned, turning to look upon Heyward.

"Yes, I am the Long Rifle!" he said, taking a confident step forward. The members of the group could not help but stare at him, shocked. Heyward was an arse, but Hawkeye could not say he was not brave. Even so, he could not allow a man to take the burden of bearing his name. So, he also stepped forward to reveal himself to the sachem.

"I am the man called *La Longue Carabine*," he said, stopping beside the major. He muttered to the officer under his breath. "Stop this Major! Only I can carry the weight of my reputation."

"Allow me this, Hawkeye. They will kill *La Longue Carabine.* Stay alive and save the ladies. Deliver them and their father to safety. I will not hold it against you. You have done so much for us..." Heyward whispered back.

Hawkeye bit his lip to keep from laughing.

How could anyone confuse Heyward for La Longue Carabine seeing the two of us side by side?

It was true enough that none of them would recognize him personally. He had never fought the Delaware, but surely they had heard of his appearance. The major was tall, around 5'10", but Hawkeye dwarfed him in size. Then there was the fact that Hawkeye was wearing the same breech-cloth as his Mohican companions, while Heyward was still in the remnants of his uniform.

As Hawkeye watched, Tamenund narrowed his gaze at both him and the major. Shouts went up from some of the Delaware spectators, who were arguing over who might be telling the truth. It truly seemed like they had no idea.

"You cannot both be *La Longue Carabine. W*hich of you is he?" the sachem demanded. However, both men protested their identity as the feared hunter, moving forward as if to encourage the sachem to believe them.

"Magua, my brother, you have claimed *La Longue Carabine* is given refuge in my camp. Which of these men is he?" Tamenund asked the Wendat. Magua said nothing, pointing a finger at Hawkeye. Heyward's eyes bulged, and he took a step toward Magua.

"Would the wise sachem believe the barking of a wolf? A dog never lies, but when has a wolf been known to speak the truth?" Heyward demanded, glaring at Magua.

"Magua, you have been called a liar," the sachem said. "Let the men shoot. Bullets have no tongues with which to deceive."

The men were both handed rifles, albeit under careful watch, and a young Delaware girl hung a pot from the branch of a tree across the clearing. Hawkeye practically glared at the major the whole time.

"Major, you cannot hope to outshoot me," Hawkeye whispered as he began to load the rifle he had received. "It is already a miracle that they believe your lie at all."

"Of course, I cannot, but you will shoot wide, allowing my stratagem to proceed without issue," Heyward responded, loading his own piece. It took everything for Hawkeye not to laugh.

"Shoot wide? I do not think I could if I wanted to, sir," Hawkeye argued. The men finished loading their guns and then focused on the pot that hung off in the distance. Heyward didn't respond. He raised his rifle, lining it up with the pot hanging in the distance.

Hawkeye watched as the man moved the rifle ever so slightly up. The major's lips parted ever so slightly as he took a deep breath. He slowly pulled the trigger.

BANG!

The pot spun, having clearly been hit, but not close enough to the center to shatter it. The Delaware then removed the gun from Heyward's grasp. All those present began chattering about the shot, but Tamenund silenced them and gestured to Hawkeye to take his turn. The scout stepped forward, looking briefly at the pot before he turned to address the Wendat chief.

"Magua, I could shoot you dead, this very second. The hawk is no more certain than the dove than I am now of you, that I might put a bullet in your heart. No power on Earth could stop me," he said, staring down the man.

"You kill me, and every one of your people here will die," Magua responded, staring him down. Hawkeye nodded and without even looking at the pot, raised his rifle and shot, throwing his rifle to the man who had given it to him immediately thereafter.

The pot fractured and shards flew in all directions, forcing those who were unfortunate enough to be standing nearby to hide their faces behind their arms. Hawkeye turned to look at Major Heyward, a small smirk playing on his lips.

"That was by chance! None can shoot without aim!" Heyward declared.

Hawkeye's posture stiffened as he looked at Heyward. "Chance? Does *Le Renard* think it chance?" He turned to the sachem. "Tamenund, give us both rifles and place us face to face, no cover! Let the Manitoo decide the matter between us!"

"Silence, Yengees!" Tamenund shouted in his quavering voice. "The hawk that comes from the crowd may come again, as he wills," the old man said, nodding toward the men holding the rifles. "Give the prisoners the rifles, and let them fire again," he ordered.

The same young Delaware girl hung another pot, though this time much farther away and the men began loading the rifles. Hawkeye's movements were quick and precise, as he had done this thousands of times. But they also had an air of annoyance, as he was being made to prove his identity, just to possibly lose his life for it.

"Go on, Major! If you are *La Longue Carabine*, break the shell of that pot," Hawkeye goaded him.

Heyward glared back at him and readied his rifle, taking his time.

Finally, he took a shallow breath and then pulled the trigger as slowly as possible. The bullet hit the tree that the pot hung from, missing its target by no more than an inch.

The crowd murmured in appreciation, and even Hawkeye gave a nod of approval. The shot was difficult; from such a distance, it would be nearly impossible to hit the target with skill alone.

"That may do for the Royal Americans, but my eye is more exact than yours! Does the woman who owns the pot own more? This one will never again hold water," Hawkeye boasted, raising his rifle to his eye and aiming at the pot, pausing for a second to look over at the group that he was fighting for. Cora had one hand balled in front of her mouth. Alice's arms were crossed, and her eyebrows were furrowed. Uncas and Chingachgook both had their hands where their knives normally sat; an instinct all three men had picked up after years of fighting. They all knew that, should he be proven as *La Longue Carabine*, the Delawares would probably kill him. Hawkeye locked eyes with Alice, who gave him a small, reassuring smile. He nodded, turned back to the pot, and fired.

The pot spun in circles, but appeared unbroken. The girl who had hung the pot searched the shell and called out that there was nary a crack on the shell of the pot.

"You are a wolf in the skin of a dog!" Tamenund shouted at Hawkeye. "Go! I will speak only with *La Longue Carabine*!" Hawkeye looked upon the sachem, undaunted.

"If I had Killdeer, I would cut the thong of the pot and drop it without breaking the pot. But I must prove my worth in other ways with this rubbish," Hawkeye motioned to the rifle that was still in his hands. "You fools must know that to find the bullet of a true American woodsman, you must look in the pot, not around it!"

The girl standing by the pot picked it up again and held it up, pointing the bottom at Tamenund.

"I can see the great sachem through it!" the girl shouted excitedly in Algonquian.

The crowd erupted into conversation about the amount of talent or luck a man would need to make a shot like that, and they all decided that it was impossible to hit it by chance.

"You are *La Longue Carabine*," Tamenund said to Hawkeye. He turned to his men. "Take him." Hawkeye did not protest, allowing two of the warriors to grab hold of his arms. Tamenund nodded at this, his eyebrows rising.

"Magua, my brother, is not a liar," the sachem said. "Magua, come forward.

The Wendat did as he was bid and took a knee before the old man. Tamenund raised his hand, motioning for Magua to stand once more.

"Why has Magua come among my people?"

"I call for justice; my prisoners are with my brother. I come for what is mine," Magua said, his voice slow and level.

"Justice is the law of the great Manitou! Huron, take your own and depart."

The Delaware men standing behind Heyward and Hawkeye bound their hands and held them firm. Magua turned to Cora to grab her, but she approached him with her head lowered. He wore a look of victory, but then she tore herself from him and threw herself at the feet of the patriarch.

"Wise and just Tamenund, on thy wisdom I plead for mercy!" She cried out. Her hands were clasped against her bosom as she looked up at the sachem from on her knees. "Hear not the twisted words of that fox; he can do no acts but evil ones!"

"What are you?" the old sachem squinted at her.

"A woman, a Yengee, one who you hate," Cora responded. "But one who has not and could never harm you. I beg you for succor!"

The old man sat for a minute, considering the woman at his feet before responding. "Tell me, my children, where have the Delaware camped?" he asked in French.

"In the mountains of the Iroquois, beyond the clear springs of Andiatarocte,[2]" Tessouat, who stood by Tamenund's side translating, responded.

"Many parching summers have come and gone since I enjoyed the waters of my own river," Tamenund reminisced. "The sons of

---

2. Andiatarocte is the name given to Lake George by the Delaware people.

Miquon[3] were the justest of the white men, but they took our river for themselves. Do you follow us so far?"

"We follow none; we covet nothing. We have been brought here as captives, against our will. We ask for nothing more than the right to depart in peace." Cora paused, thinking, before continuing. "Are you not Tamenund—the father, the judge of his people?"

"I am Tamenund of many days," the old man responded. He gazed at the collection of Delawares and prisoners before him. "It was just yesterday that the children of the Lenape were the masters of the world. The fish of the salt lake, the birds, the beasts of the woods saluted the sagamores before their own."

Cora looked at her hands. "Is Tamenund a father?"

"Of a nation."

"For myself, I ask nothing, great sachem. But look upon my father," Cora said, motioning toward the old man who stood helpless beside his younger daughter. "This man whom I have just been reunited with. He is my father, Tamenund. Would you take me from him and deliver me into the hands of a greedy fox who only wants me for some sick game of revenge?" she entreated, looking over at her captor with contempt.

Tamenund ignored her question and continued his great speech from before. "I know that the white men are a proud and hungry race. I know that they believe the meanest of them to be better than the wisest sagamores," he said, earning calls of approval from his audience. "The dogs and crows of their tribes would bark and caw before they

---

3. Miquon was the name given to William Penn by the Lenape, in reference to the Lenape word for quill—the Lenape and Penn signed the Treaty of Shackamaxon.

took into their wigwams a woman whose blood was not the color of snow."

Cora bit her lip, and glanced at her father before facing the sachem again. "Not so!" She gestured for her father to take a step forward, and he obliged her. "Look upon this man, my father, who sired two children with the granddaughter of a negro slave." Few sounds were heard upon this revelation, aside from the gasps of those in the colonel's own party. Major Heyward backed away from the man, eyeing Alice with horrified eyes. Alice covered her mouth with her hand.

Tamenund met Cora's eyes, his own full of disappointment. "You think this evidence of your virtue, but the reactions of your kin have shown the truth of my words."

Cora looked back at her father, a tear forming in the corner of her eyes as she realized that this was a hopeless endeavor.

"But let them not boast in the face of the Manitoo too loud! They came in at the rising, and may yet go away at the setting of the sun. I have often seen the locusts strip the leaves from the trees," he pondered. "But the seasons of the flowers always come again."

"If you will not listen to a Yengee, hear the voice of your own," Cora replied, no longer arguing with the old sachem.

Tamenund's gaze swept over those present. "Who would speak for you?"

"He who does can be no more than a snake!" Tessouat declared. "An Indian in the pay of the Yengees. We will keep he who steps forward for the torture!"

"Let him come to my feet," Tamenund countered. The room was quiet for a few moments while there was no motion. Then, Uncas emerged from the group. He stood in front of the great sachem, glancing around at the crowd before his face settled, looking upon Tamenund.

"With what tongue does the prisoner speak to the Manitoo?" Tamenund demanded.

"With the tongue of my fathers, Algonquian," Uncas responded, squaring his shoulders for the response this comment would earn. Those in the surrounding crowd began cursing at him and trying to get closer to hiss and spit on him.

"A Delaware?" Tamenund questioned. "I have lived to see the council fires of my people scattered about the hills of the Iroquois. I have seen the hatchets of strange people sweep the trees from the valleys that the winds of the heavens had spared, but I have never seen a Delaware so base as to creep, like a snake, into the camps of his fathers!"

"The wolves have opened their mouths, and Tamenund would hear their howls," Uncas replied.

The old sage leaned in to hear these words clearer as if he could not believe what the young man was saying. "Does Tamenund dream? What voice is at his ears? Have the winters gone backward? Will summer come again to the people of the Turtle?"

Tessouat sneered at Uncas. "The false Delaware would tremble, lest he hear the words of Tamenund! He is a hound that howls when the Yengees show him a trail!"

"And you are dogs that whine when the Frenchman cast you the antlers of his deer!" Uncas shouted at the sagamore. Those in the area immediately responded by pulling out their knives to attack the young Mohican.

Uncas could see Cora in the corner, a hand placed against her chest, concern etched across her face. He nodded to her. *Just trust me,* he entreated with his eyes.

"A Delaware? You are unworthy of the name! The warrior who deserts his tribe when it is hidden by the clouds is doubly a traitor. The law of the Manitoo is just!" Tamenund motioned for Tessouat to help him rise, and he stood to leave. "It is so; while the rivers run and the mountains stand, it must be so! My children, he is thine, do justly by him." Tessouat helped Tamenund off his chair to leave.

At least six pairs of hands attempted to seize Uncas, but he thrashed around to avoid their grasp. If he was going to die, he refused to do so without a fight, not with Cora so close.

"He shall die by the fire!" Tessouat shouted.

One of the hands that reached for his shoulder got caught on the medallion that hung around his neck and ripped it from his body. Suddenly, the perpetrator pulled away, ceasing his attack. He muttered something in Algonquian and pointed at Uncas' chest.

There was a tattoo in the middle of the Mohican's chest. It was a turtle, tinted blue, about the size of a strawberry. Those who had been attacking him just seconds ago looked on in awe. The blue turtle was a totem reserved for those of the oldest blood. The only men alive with the same tattoo were Uncas' father and the great sachem Tamenund.

"How could your fire harm me?" Uncas demanded, his eyes flashing. "My blood alone would smother it. My race is the grandfather of nations!"

"Who are you?" Tamenund demanded.

"I am Uncas, son of Chingachgook! I..." Uncas beckoned his father over, whose own tattoo was now in clear view. "...We are the sons of the great Unamis.[4] I am a Mohican."

Tamenund lifted a shaky hand to cover his mouth. He looked upon the young man in front of him and then up at the sky.

"The hour of Tamenund is nigh! The night has come at last, and the Manitoo has sent one to fill my place at the council fire! Let the eyes of the dying eagle gaze upon the rising sun!" He then looked upon the elder Mohican. "And you? You bear the mark as well. Who is your father?"

"I am the father and son of Uncas," Chingachgook replied, his shoulders back and chin high.

"So it is true! I remember Uncas, the panther of his tribe! But why did he leave? Why has your place at the council fire been so long empty?"

"Once we slept where we could hear the salt lake speak in anger, but then the white men came. A Yengee could be seen at every brook, and we went back into the woods. The white man's war tore us apart, and eventually, all who came with us died, save Chingachgook," Uncas motioned toward his father, "...and Uncas, his son."

"Uncas is gone? How did my friend die?" Tamenund asked, swallowing and looking at the ground.

"The disease took my grandfather," Uncas said quietly. "But after the disease and white men plagued our nation, it was just my father and I left. We wanted no part in the war, so we did not return."

"It is true! My wise men have told me that two men of the unchanged race roam the hillside of the Hudson!"

---

4. "Unamis" is the word for turtle in the Lenape tongue.

"Not two, but three, my father!" Uncas replied to the patriarch. He brought Hawkeye forward, still bound, to stand in front of the sachem. "I bid you, father, look upon this white man! He is brave and just, feared by the Hurons, and a friend of the Delawares!"

"What name has this white man earned for his actions?"

"We call him Hawkeye," Uncas said. "For his aim is so exact. But the Hurons would know him by the weapon with which he kills: the long rifle."

"*La Longue Carabine*! My son does not well to call him friend!"

"I call him so who proves himself such. If Uncas is welcome among the Delawares, so is Hawkeye, his brother."

"Brother?"

"Aye, brother. My father found this young pup dying in the cabin of his parents. They were slain by the Hurons," Uncas said, glancing at Magua. The Wendat chief was frozen, the only movement he made was a slight twitch of his nose.

"My father was raising Hawkeye before I was even born. If he is not Chingachgook's son, neither am I."

"He has slain the Lenape; how could you call him brother?" Tamenund asked.

Hawkeye interjected, cutting off his brother's retort. "If the great Tamenund has heard that, his ears must have heard the wolf's howls. I have killed many Hurons in my day, I would not deny it even in front of their own sachems, but my hand has never knowingly harmed a Delaware. I am a friend to all who are friends of my family."

Tamenund nodded. "And where is the Huron?" he demanded. Magua stepped forward, scowling at the scout and his brother as he passed them to take a knee once more before the sachem.

"The just Tamenund would not keep what Magua has lent. Give me my prisoners and let me go."

"Tell me, my son," Tamenund addressed Uncas again. "Has the Huron conquerors rights over you?"

"He has none. Traps he may have set, but the deer can escape the traps of little boys."

"Over *La Longue Carabine*?"

Uncas gave a mocking laugh. "None. Magua should ask his young warriors the color of a bear."

"The white men and the light-haired woman that came with you into my camp?"

"None!"

"And the woman? The dark-haired woman?"

Uncas made no reply.

"The woman? The woman the Huron brought into my camp?" Tamenund repeated.

"She is mine," Magua said, glancing back at the girl in question. "You cannot argue that she is mine!"

Cora's family looked on in shock that Uncas would not defend Cora.

"So she is," Uncas responded.

"Very well," the sachem said, his voice grave. He gestured to Magua. "Huron, depart!"

"No, please, wise Tamenund!" Cora begged as several of the Delaware warriors pushed her into the arms of her captor.

"You are his, woman; depart and find a life of peace with him. Your race will not end."

"Better a thousand times that it did!" she cried out.

Tamenund looked down upon the scene from his chair, pursing his lips.

"Magua, her heart is not with you. An unwilling wife makes for an unhappy wigwam."

"She is mine! I will take her," Magua said, resolutely.

Tamenund gave a heavy sigh.

"Then depart with your own."

"Wait!" Hawkeye's voice rang out and Magua turned, scowling. "Huron, you...I will go with you... You may have me; take my rifle for your own, but leave the woman!"

Magua's head jerked back at the offer. There was a gleam in his eyes as he beheld the scout.

"No, Hawkeye, you will not! I refuse to be a part of such a deal!" Cora shouted, pleading with Hawkeye to retract his offer. Magua looked between Cora and Hawkeye, his eyes finally settling on the girl in his arms.

"No, I will take my revenge with this woman!" he shouted, dragging her toward the exit. He paused beside her father, who was held back by Delawares.

"Know that your daughter will spend the rest of her life as my woman, Munro. She will cook my food and warm my bed. And you can go to your grave knowing your grandchildren will be half Huron!" Magua crowed to the ashen-faced old man.

Munro went crazy, pulling hard at the men holding him. He cursed at the Wendat, who half carried a protesting Cora away from the crowd toward the woods.

43
Wendat Camp
08:34

Magua had a hand wrapped around Cora's arm, pulling her in the direction of his village. A small part of him wanted to gloat after getting what he wanted, but he was beginning to realize he had no desire to hurt the woman. If he ever hoped for her to love him, he would need to separate her from her father in his head.

"We are nearly there, my dear. Just ten more minutes and we shall have our protection."

"Magua please! You must have some empathy in your frozen heart!" the girl protested, ignoring his comment. "How can you do this to me? You are a good man inside, I know you are. You have just been perverted by your hatred of my father, which I understand, but doing this will hurt me more than him. Please, Magua!" she begged him, tugging on his arm.

"Your father's time will come, Cora, but I desire him to die with a broken heart. If I simply killed him, he would find peace in death, but the thought of you submitting to me, and worse, bearing such *savage* children, will torture him even in death."

Cora's eyes flashed. "You are a monster! You would steal me away from my sister, force me into a life with you, surrounded by people I do not know, people who have killed my friends, and all for the benefit of a man whom you will kill? Why? Can you not simply tell him you will do these things, and then let me be after he is dead?"

Magua pulled the girl toward him, forcing her to look him in the eyes as he uttered every painful word. "Every night, when my scars ache, I can feel the whip piercing me over and over and over again! I can hear your father's laughter as he cut my back up. And then..." the Wendat chief took a shaky breath as if the memories themselves were paining him. "...and then I can hear the screams of my family. I see them beating my father to death; I can still see the look on my mother's face as your father drew his sword before he..." he stuttered, not finishing the thought. "My sisters, lying broken on the ground, begging for death after what your father allowed his men to do to them! Do you think your father deserves mercy for that? Do you think that devil should have any reprieve from his pain? Why can you not understand the mercy I am giving him by not murdering his children?" Magua demanded, wiping the back of his hand across his eyes as he dragged Cora along through his painful memories.

The girl was quiet for a moment, not responding. He began pulling her with him again.

"My heart breaks for you, Magua. I have never felt so horrible for another person in my life. He did you wrong. But that was him, not me." She was silent for a moment. "Is there any part of you that feels for me, that understands how you are hurting me?" She asked, her voice quiet and tender.

Magua came to a stop right outside his village and held Cora by both arms, forcing her to meet his eyes. "Understand me now, woman; I do not want to hurt you. This is not about you. Please try to understand why you must take the brunt of his punishment. I will be a good husband. You need not fear my wrath. I will never hurt you or force anything on you, and I will protect you," he said. He tried to make his voice softer, less intimidating, but he knew nothing he did would appease her.

She looked up at him, her eyes glistening.

Sighing, he led her into the camp. Several women were busy at work in the camp, but their eyes followed the pair.

Magua opened the door to a longhouse and brought her inside, where he released her arm. This was the longhouse where Uncas had been kept prisoner. There were four Wendat chiefs seated at the back of the room. They were talking to each other when Magua joined them.

"I pay my honors to the sachem and chiefs of the Wendat," Magua said in Wyandot, lowering his head to acknowledge their authority. The chiefs likewise inclined their heads to appreciate Magua's authority. The sachem in the middle nodded toward the carpet, for Magua to take a seat. Magua obliged him, Cora still standing behind him.

"You have a different woman now, Magua. What has come to pass?"

"The light-haired woman escaped with the British officer. They have schemed to take away my dark-haired prisoner, but Magua is a fox, not a dumb rabbit. Magua brings his prisoner to the safety of the Wendat camp," Magua said.

The sachem frowned. "Safety? Are the woods unsafe, even to such a wise chief?"

Magua bit the inside of his mouth. "The Delaware will be on my trail in only a few hours."

"The Delaware?" The sachem shifted position on the carpet. "Are we not at peace with these Turtle?"

"So we were, but they have turned against us, and against Montcalm," Magua said. "When I went to retrieve my prisoner, I quarreled with the Mohicans; *Le Gros Serpent,* and *Le Cerf Agile. Le Cerf Agile* revealed himself to be a descendant of the sachem Tamenund's friend. The Turtle supported *Le Cerf Agile* when he declared war on me."

"War on you, Magua, but not war on us. Why should we allow you to remain here? You bring an advancing force that would harm our village."

Magua shook his head. "I have done nothing to provoke these people, save request my own prisoner. They are like foolish women, and we should put them in their place."

"Magua is a great chief," one of the chiefs argued. "If the Delaware come, they come for all of us, and we cannot allow this disrespect." The rest of the chiefs agreed, and the sachem nodded.

"Very well, we must prepare."

44
Duncan Heyward

10:01

C olonel Munro's head throbbed. He was getting too old for war, and he was certainly too old to be running about the wilderness in search of his daughter. However, Magua needed to pay and Cora needed to be rescued. Now, for reasons beyond Munro, the Delaware were intent on waiting until the sun rose to go after Magua and his men. Even Chingachgook was insistent that they should only depart when ready for war.

The blanket draped over the entrance to Colonel Munro's wigwam was pushed aside and Major Heyward entered. He greeted the colonel with a perfunctory bow, his lips drawn in a thin line.

"I would like to discuss your daughter, sir."

"Oh, you would? Have you thought of a brilliant plan to rescue her?" the colonel asked with an edge to his voice. He could already sense what the major was intending to talk about.

"Not remotely," the man replied, his voice laced with annoyance. "They are both...besmirched by Negro blood?"

The colonel pushed himself to his feet. "Indeed they are. My wife was a beautiful woman, not least because of her lovely complexion. She was genteel, the daughter of a gentleman and a lady. Her name was Elizabeth Ives and she resembled my dear Cora very much, albeit with somewhat darker skin. When I met Elizabeth's mother, I was, in truth, shocked. Upon asking Elizabeth, she clarified what I had already surmised; she was the descendant of a black slave. Cora and Alice's great-grandmother was a slave, and I'm told a beautiful woman whose abuse at the hands of her owner had resulted in the birth of my daughters' grandmother." Colonel Munro could see the sneer forming on the major's face, but he continued with the story. "I knew all of this when I married Elizabeth and when she gave me two beautiful daughters. I am not regretful of my actions. I may have believed those unfortunate souls were less than us at one point, but one conversation with Elizabeth destroyed that belief. That is what love can do. So, dear boy, are you to insult an aging man's offspring to his face? I know you are from the South where those with darker skin than ours are enslaved, so tell me, Duncan, how deep does your prejudice lie?"

Duncan's face contorted in both loathing and disgust.

"You, sir, should be embarrassed by what you have brought into your house. And to deceive honest folk; to let those around you form connections with those *creatures*, with no knowledge..."

"Oh, no knowledge! How can they be so low if you had no knowledge of it? You are so confident to come and hate my daughters, yet if I had said nothing, you would think no differently. My daughters are ladies. But fear not, I believe these connections you speak of were entirely one-sided to begin with. You could never deserve the affections of my daughter!" Munro shouted, slapping the man across the face.

Heyward's eyes blazed as he raised his own hand for a brief second before lowering it.

"Get out of my sight," Munro said through gritted teeth.

Heyward stormed out of the wigwam and began yelling for someone to bring him a horse. Munro watched as the soldier rode off, not even casting a glance over his shoulder as he left the village.

45
Fit for a Bride

15:52

Cora stood in the longhouse, wringing her hands as she stared at the door. She could hear the men outside readying for the fight. Glancing out the crack in the door, she saw women running around, handing water skins to the men, who were getting in a quick meal before they set out. She backed up and reached for the canteen that Magua had left her, hoping to calm herself with a drink.

Her eyes trailed over to the flowers that adorned every inch of the longhouse. She was unsure why they were there, but almost magically over a hundred flowers were scattered in the hut. They were different colors, but there were many more red flowers than any other colors.

The door to the longhouse flew open and Magua walked in, his eyes blazing with adrenaline. Cora looked up at him, her face a mask of resolve while her heart pounded in her chest. She wore the buckskin dress he had gotten for her. It was heavily adorned with beading. She had a red headband on her head with lengths of twisted red string hanging in her black hair. She looked more beautiful than ever.

"You are to leave now?" she questioned.

Magua grinned from ear to ear.

"I will soon enough, but you can be certain that I will return soon. And I will come bearing wedding gifts..." he said, laughing at his own joke before boasting, "The scalp of your father and Uncas shall be yours, my dear!"

"You'll have to kill them first, Magua." Cora argued, taking steps toward the villain as her voice rose. "My father survived your first bloody scrimmage. He will survive another, and no one can kill *Le Cerf Agile*. You know you cannot kill him, Huron. He's as fast as the hind for which he is named."

"Can't I? Speed is a very important quality, my dear, but wits, the wits of a fox, will always win." He had an infuriating smirk on his face.

"Wits? You cannot call your dishonorable actions wit! How much wit did it take for you to organize the killing of all those women at Henry?" she rebuked him.

Magua rolled his eyes. "Honor? You'd lecture me on honor? What says your father of the honor of whipping his subordinates? The man who holds his honor loses his head!"

"Not so! Uncas is an honorable man, and he lives still!"

"You think so highly of the Mohican, yet he has killed just like me! He is a murderer, Cora. How can you defend his honor? Will Uncas answer for the deaths of my young men in the village, or at Glen?"

"Not all killing is dishonorable," Cora stated resolutely, shaking her head. "The men that Uncas has slain were either attacking him or holding him hostage!"

"A man of honor would have died in my village before killing his young guards. Ennons had not seen seventeen summers!"

Cora looked at the ground before continuing. "If the only thing at risk was Uncas' life, he would have gladly died, but my own life was and still is in the balance. Uncas would protect me from your evil plan!"

Magua did not respond, only held his lips in a thin line. The girl's arguments tore at his heart. It pained him to hurt such a good person. Deep down, he believed that some part of his plan of taking her to wife was out of revenge for her father, but he could not pretend there were no feelings involved. He cared deeply for Cora.

"Can you at least understand why this is not right, Magua?" Cora demanded of him, her voice soft now, her eyes beseeching him.

Magua didn't respond, only stepped toward the door to leave. Then he turned back and spoke quickly, "I must leave to retrieve your wedding gifts." Cora broke down in tears, falling to her knees, her arms wrapped around herself.

46
Birds
16:18

A lice watched Heyward walk into the wigwam her father resided in and then storm out a few minutes later. She pondered on what the two of them had discussed, because Heyward threw himself onto a horse and left in a hurry. She wondered if she would ever see him again.

She was sitting in the wigwam with all the ladies of the village, preparing for the impending fight. They were wrapping fetching on the arrows they were assembling. One of the women had taught Alice the process; she had picked it up quite fast; as her nimble fingers were used to the type of artistry that was required.

Most of the women did not speak much English, although the generally spoke some French, which Alice could work around clumsily. They chattered about meaningless things, but their curt voices and furrowed brows showed their anxiety. The tension in the air was palpable. The Wendats were fierce fighters; they were sure to put up a hard fight.

Alice understood the women's anxiety; she was nervous about what could happen to those men who were important to her. Her father was old, yet insisted on fighting, and Hawkeye...

The man himself walked into the wigwam. All the Delaware ladies looked up from their work, surprised, and then they all began greeting him in Algonquian. Alice noticed that the women seemed giddy with Hawkeye in the wigwam. They put down the arrows they were working on and crowded around him, giggling and asking him questions that Alice couldn't understand, and touching him on the arm and chest. Their eyes were glued to the man.

Hawkeye smiled at the ladies, answering their questions and shooting glances at Alice every couple of seconds, giving her a knowing smirk. She couldn't help but grin. The man was downright addictive; Alice understood the ladies' excitement.

After greeting them all, he made it through the crowd to Alice. She put down the arrow she was working on as he approached her.

"They've got you working on arrows, Alice?" he questioned, offering her a hand to help her up. She nodded, accepting his hand.

"If there's anything I can do to help in my sister's rescue, I will," she said, determined. He nodded at this comment, with an expression akin to pride.

"And to think you do not find yourself brave," he said. She looked at the ground, her cheeks brightening.

"I guess I realize now that I am, in my own little way..."

"Alice...Could we talk for a minute?"

"Of course." She allowed Hawkeye to lead her out of the wigwam toward the edge of the village. She gazed up at him as she followed him.

"Yes, Hawkeye?"

"I..." he began confidently but lost his words as he looked into her eyes, shimmering in the light. "...I just wanted to check and see how you are. Everyone has been so worried about how your father is dealing with it. They just expect you to cope perfectly for some reason..." he trailed off.

She cocked her head to the side. "You want to hear the truth?" she asked. He nodded, encouraging her with his eyes. "I'm terrified. I worry that at any point someone is going to tell me that my sister, the only person I've been able to rely on my whole life, is dead, or worse, has been defiled by the monster who took her from me. And selfishly, I am frightened that the Hurons will overcome this village and kill me, and I'm so young, I'm so…" The lady started breathing heavily, putting a hand to her chest in an effort to calm herself.

Hawkeye took hold of her hand and rubbed circles on it. He drew her against him, wrapping his arms around her quivering body, and held her tight. She buried her head in his chest and tried to slow her breathing as he whispered in her ear.

"Shhhh, everything is going to be alright. Uncas will save your sister, and even if this camp fell, I would never let anyone harm you. I will protect you, always," he said.

She wrapped her arms tight around his torso, as she sobbed against him.

"What if she dies, Hawkeye? What will I do without her? And what of my father? How can he survive if his daughter dies? What can I do? I am lost!"

Hawkeye rubbed her back with one hand and held her head against his chest with the other, slowing down his breathing so that she might calm herself against him.

"Take deep breaths, my sweet. You will be alright. I will stay with you, Alice. No man will harm you while I live, and should your family fall, you may follow me into the woods," he said. At this she calmed, her tears stopping. She pulled back, her heart still beating erratically from panic, and looked up at him.

"Truly?"

"I swear it. You need only ask and you can follow me to the ends of the Earth," he reassured her. Another tear fell and she pressed herself back to his chest as she thanked him.

"If Cora lives and I still have a family, will I still see you?"

"Does the lady wish for me to stay? I am at her disposal."

Alice looked at her feet again, blushing. "Hawkeye, I think...I would like to follow you, after this is all over, if my family lives, I mean...I still...I've come to feel..." She couldn't seem to form the sentence that she wanted to say.

"Shh...I understand what you mean, my dear. You will always be welcome at my side," he said.

She gave him a small smile, not knowing how to respond. He grinned back at her and leaned down to plant a small kiss on her forehead.

"I should...get back to making arrows..." she said, stumbling over her words.

"Very well."

Alice squeezed his hand, then scurried back to the wigwam. Just before she ducked inside, she turned and gave him a beaming smile, laying a hand on her heart.

13 August 1757

47
The Battle

17:59

Uncas' Delaware army crept through the trees. He had urged them to stay behind cover when possible because once they broke the tree line, they would be visible to the attacking Hurons. Uncas made eye contact with his brother, who was across the way, leading his own group of Delaware, Killdeer in his hands once again.

He nodded, and Hawkeye returned the nod. The scout shouted and gestured to the men in his group to follow him down the side of the hill toward the Wendats. Seconds later, Magua gave an answering war cry, and the two groups began fighting.

Hawkeye discharged a shot and then it was all hand-to-hand combat. He had brought a club with him, which he swung around, felling any man who dared come near him. Magua was fighting some twenty yards away, and the men made eye contact, subconsciously getting closer to each other.

The battlefield was still filled with musket smoke, though only a few men were still firing. The screams of men filled in the gaps between shots so that the battlefield was constantly deafening.

Once the groups had been fighting for a few minutes, Chingachgook, whose group was hiding in the woods opposite Hawkeye's group, raced down the hill, flanking Magua's men and forcing them to fight in two directions.

Magua thrust his knife into an attacking Delaware's gut and dragged it across his belly, spilling the man's intestines. The man screamed and reached down to try and scoop them up. At the touch of his insides, he collapsed, his eyes closing.

Hawkeye, an equally skilled fighter, was making good progress against the Wendats. Most of the men cowered on seeing *La Longue Carabine*. He tore through all his enemies easily and without a blade. Any Wendat foolish enough to approach him was clubbed to death before they could ever get within arm's length of him. Soon, he was surrounded by the mangled bodies of his victims, their heads mostly disfigured and unrecognizable.

Two Delaware rushed Magua, both double-wielding a knife and a tomahawk. He ducked and rolled under the slice of one, swinging his own hatchet backward to slash the man in the back. As he was wrenching his hatchet free, the other Delaware took the opportunity to dive at him. Magua was able to jut to the side, but the man's knife still caught his side, leaving a shallow gash there. He flipped his knife around in his hand so that he held it by the blade, then threw it into the Delaware's gut. The man crumpled to the ground, gripping the knife.

With his hatchet now fully free from the back of his first victim, Magua approached the second man and grabbed the knife. He stared the man in the eyes as he twisted it and dragged it up through the man's chest.

Breathing hard, Magua stood and looked down at the bloody gash on his side. This was going to be harder than he thought. His eyes flitted around the battlefield, searching for the men he had promised to kill. The colonel was easy enough to find; he was fighting right beside Chingachgook, using his cavalry sword. Magua shook his head at the colonel's stupidity.

Cavalry swords were a little under three feet long. They were very useful for attacking enemy fighters on the ground when you were mounted on a horse, but in this thick fighting where everyone was so close together, it took a long time for the aged man to recover after a swing.

He sprinted toward the man, dodging blows and slashes from other erratic Delaware warriors. The colonel saw him coming. He stabbed the man he was fighting and turned to face the Wendat chief.

"Come here, you rodent, so that I may do what I do best: kill filthy savages," the old man snarled.

"You think you can kill me? You needed three men just to beat me. Pathetic," Magua said, his knife gleaming in the scorching August sun.

The old man swung his sword at Magua, but the Wendat ducked and rolled to the side. He dove at the old man, but Munro blocked him out of the way with the butt of his sword, throwing Magua to the ground once. However, the Wendat was on his feet in a flash.

The colonel swung his sword at Magua, who once again ducked, this time charging him low while he was recovering from the previous swing. Magua's knife was swallowed by Munro's belly and the old officer staggered back a step, crying out in agony. Magua pulled the knife back out and stood back to admire his handiwork. Munro's eyes were frantic, jumping back and forth between the Wendat chief and the injury he had sustained.

Magua looked at the man with crazed eyes, barely able to believe that his dream was finally coming true. He had thought of nothing else for the last nine years. He had fallen asleep every night, picturing himself killing the colonel in different ways; relishing the pain he would inflict on him when he had the chance.

When Magua met the colonel's daughters for the first time, he thought he had found a new way to harm the old man. Initially, he had considered killing the girls, but he was better than the old colonel. He would not harm others to take his revenge.

He took a step toward the old man, who flailed his sword weakly, while clutching at his wound with the other hand. However, Magua easily caught the blade in the crook of his hatchet and wrenched it from the colonel's hand. The sword fell to the ground at his feet.

Munro looked up at him, one hand raised as if to hold Magua off, then groaned as he fell onto his back. Magua leapt forward, crouching beside the old man. Munro had one bloody hand covering his wound, while he punched the ground hard with the other.

"I will tell you the future, swine," Magua snarled as he pulled a special knife from his satchel. "You are going to die, desperate and alone on this battlefield. I am going to take your scalp, and I will make it a wedding gift to your daughter. She will be my woman and she will lie with me every day for the rest of her life. Go to the grave with the knowledge that your grandchildren will be half Huron!"

The old man groaned in pain. He was thrashing around at this point, his body convulsing as blood poured from his stomach. His eyes bulged. Laughing in triumph, Magua brought the edge of his knife to the colonel's hairline. It barely broke the old man's skin before he began cursing the Wendat savagely.

"You'll burn in hell for this, you disgusting heathen!"

"Then I'll see you there," Magua said calmly as he dragged his knife under the man's skin. The old man cried out, blood from the wound pouring down the side of his face. Magua continued to drag his knife down the length of the colonel's head, separating the man's scalp from his skull. The colonel was screaming at this point. Magua had the mind to stay there and enjoy the man's pain for a bit longer, but he could not waste the time. He brought his knife up and shoved it into Munro's heart. The old man's eyebrows scrunched together before his eyes fluttered closed and his face finally relaxed. Magua tied the scalp to his side and rose to his feet. He wiped his hands on his vest with a satisfied smile.

His head on a swivel, Magua looked around the battlefield at all the attacking Delawares. He was eerily calm, and the Turtle that saw him cowered at his stoicism. Magua scanned for the young Mohican he was sure would be leading the attack. However, *Le Cerf Agile* was nowhere to be found. It was then that Magua realized what was happening.

A triumphant shout erupted from the top of the hill, and a Delaware force, fifty-strong, came rushing down the hill. Uncas was leading them. The Wendats looked up in horror at the incoming force and began milling around and panicking. Some managed to rush back toward the village from which they had come, but many were already engaged in fighting and could not escape.

Magua, realizing that he could not win the fight, called three nearby warriors to follow him, and they raced back toward the Wendat camp. He was determined to get to Cora before the attacking Delawares.

They entered the village and Magua went straight to the longhouse where Cora was being held. He threw the blanket aside and looked down on the girl he had fought so hard to keep. Her eyes were red and swollen. She had obviously been crying.

"Stand, woman. We need to leave!" he shouted at her. She nodded, rising to her feet. She began brushing the dirt off her clothing and reached down to get a drink from the water skin he had left her, but Magua was in a hurry. He grabbed her arm and dragged her out of the longhouse. Once they were outside, he reached into his satchel with his other hand and pulled out the scalp.

As her eyes fixed on it, she let out a horrified scream. He shoved it into her hand and pulled her close to him, bringing his lips to her ear.

"The scalp of your father, just as I promised!" he growled.

She sobbed and fell to her knees. Dropping the hideous trophy, she wrapped her arms around the Wendat chief's leg.

"How could you do this? Why must you hurt me so? WHY?" she shouted. Magua looked down at the girl, his face screwed up in frustration. He had never wished Cora harm, but it was the only way to achieve the vengeance he had sought for so long.

"Come! We must go!" He dragged her to her feet and pulled her behind him. She staggered, barely able to walk in her grief. This time, he picked her up, slung her over his back, and began running away from the camp.

Cora pounded her fists on Magua's back.

"You only have one scalp! Uncas is alive! He shall come for me and kill you!" she shouted as the man ran up a path on the mountain. "I hate you! I hate you! I hate you!" However, Magua did not respond, internalizing everything to deal with it later when he and his prize were safe.

The three men Magua had called to follow him took turns carrying the girl, and they made good progress, getting farther and farther away while the men pursuing Cora had not even reached the Wendat village yet.

48
The Final Fight

14:11

M agua dragged Cora along the rock ledge, his three men trailing them. She had no idea where they were going; they seemed to be escaping, but Magua had promised vengeance on Uncas. Her father's blood still stained her hands, but surely Uncas could survive. He was young and able to fight off Magua; her aging father had not been strong enough.

She kept tripping, as the long buckskin dress inhibited her full range of motion. Magua's hand was around her wrist as he dragged her along. He barely looked at her, seemingly unmoved if she scraped herself trying to match his pace. Suddenly, Cora's foot caught on a small ledge and she fell to her hands and knees. She winced, feeling the rock cut into her knees and the blood seeping into her clothing. However, Magua just wrenched her arm and pulled her to her feet. Her shoulder erupted in pain and she cried out, clutching it with her other arm.

"Faster, woman! Your Mohican is getting closer."

"All the better that he is!" Cora said, wrenching her wrist from his hand. Beads of sweat dripped down her face as she sucked in lungfuls of air, staring him down.

The three men studied them from the cliff above. Uncas held his bow, the arrow already fixed to the sinew string, intending to pick off Magua's men individually. The thought that Magua might attempt to cut his losses and just kill Cora crossed Uncas' mind, but he pushed it down, reassuring himself that he could not save the girl without ridding her of her captors.

"You will follow me; you are mine!" Magua shouted into Cora's face. But she turned away from him.

"You follow me or you die!" Magua repeated. This time, Cora nodded, trudging on behind him. Suddenly, a cry came from the man at the back. He clutched his chest where an arrow protruded. Magua cursed and pulled Cora along. "Move, woman!"

"Must we keep the woman with us?" one of Magua's men questioned him in Wyandot.

"Anyone who touches her will lose his life," Magua snapped.

Cora followed on, tripping as the ground grew ever steeper and rugged. Her foot caught on a rock, and she fell to her hands and knees once again. She pushed herself to her feet, fire in her eyes. Chingachgook and Hawkeye stood some ten yards behind Uncas on the ridge above, their rifles trained on Magua's men.

"I will go no further!" Cora stated, "Kill me if you will, but I will go no further!" She clenched her fists and glared at Magua as he turned back, his face red with fury.

"Choose, Cora! Me or my knife. You must choose one!" he shouted, his voice breaking as he did. His desperation was evident. Unbeknownst to him, Uncas sat, perched over them, ready to pounce the second Magua moved toward the woman he loved.

"It is Uncas, Magua; it has always been Uncas," she said, her voice level and clear, her chin high in the face of so much danger. Magua's hand shook, barely able to keep hold of his knife.

"Choose!" His eyes pleaded with her. Cora could see the struggle and the pain. If the man had not shoved the bloody scalp of her father into her hand just two hours before, she might have felt some pity for him. It was evident that he did not want to kill her. She stepped back, away from him.

"I have chosen." Her voice was resolute.

Magua's face screwed up with frustration, and he raised his knife above his head quickly. He searched her face for any signs of her giving in, but he found none. Still, he hesitated, unable to bring himself to kill this woman.

Uncas, noticing Magua lift his knife but missing his moment of hesitation, sprang from the cliff and landed on the Wendat chief. Magua fell under the weight of Uncas' attack, and the two grappled. The other man whom Magua had brought along seized the opportunity to grab Cora by the wrist, bringing his knife toward her chest.

Before his evil plan could come to fruition, a shot rang out. It missed the man but forced him away from the lady. Chingachgook dropped the musket he had shot and leapt down onto the ground, standing between Cora and the man who had attempted to kill her. He seized his hatchet and knife, readying himself to fight. The Wendat snarled, robbed of his plan.

Chingachgook made quick work of the man, side-stepping his knife and pulling his arm behind his back. He shoved it upwards until he heard a snap. Then he brought his knife up and drew it across the man's throat, leaving the Wendat choking on his own blood.

Magua heaved Uncas off him, and the young Mohican hit the cliff side hard. Seizing the brief window of opportunity, Magua turned on Chingachgook, who leaned over the man he had killed, wiping the blood off his knife.

"Father!" Uncas cried out.

The warning was not quick enough to warn Chingachgook of the man behind him, who thrust his knife into Chingachgook's back. The sagamore's back arched and he cried out. Hawkeye fired Killdeer, but Magua jerked to the side, protecting himself from the shot.

Magua retracted his knife, throwing Chingachgook to the ground. Then he turned on Uncas. The man pushed himself to his feet, tears welling in his eyes. Magua knew he had less than a minute until *La Longue Carabine* reloaded. He stalked toward Uncas, smirking at him.

"Be ready to meet your father in death, Mohican," Magua taunted. Uncas' eyes were crazed as he held his knife up, ready to fight the villain.

Cora threw herself on the ground beside Chingachgook. She sobbed, taking his hand in hers as she begged.

"Great sagamore, you must not perish!"

"Do not cry, my child. I see before me the only woman who is worthy of my son. Do by him justly," Chingachgook said, smiling weakly up at her.

"But why must you die? What? For me? Why would you give your life for me?" she questioned him.

"I have always known I would leave Uncas one day, and I can now be certain he will have a family. Farewell Tëmetët, tell my dear Chulëntët that I say goodbye," the man said, pressing a knife into Cora's hand. She glanced down at the handle, which contained a new family portrait. There was now a small bird flying alongside the hawk from before, and a wolf danced with the stag in perfect harmony.

Cora sobbed and kept begging him to survive as Uncas began to fight *Le Renard Subtil*. Magua swung his hatchet at the Mohican, who ducked out of the way and dove, his knife biting Magua's side. Magua growled and spun, facing Uncas again.

Uncas charged him and went to stab him from above. Grunting, Magua caught his wrist and swung his hatchet, but Uncas caught his wrist as well. The two struggled against each other now; the only thing keeping them apart was their equally incredible strength.

Magua swept a leg under Uncas, which sent him reeling against the rock face. Magua could hear Hawkeye loading his rifle; he was almost finished. All Uncas would have to do was get out of the way, and Hawkeye would have a free shot. So he leapt on the Mohican, swinging his hatchet at him.

Uncas dove to the side, and Magua's hatchet hit the rock face hard, sending a shockwave through his body that made him drop his hatchet. He snatched it with his left hand, trying to shake out his right to rid it of the vibration from the attack.

From the ground, Uncas kicked Magua in the stomach, pushing him away from him. Magua fell on his back, which gave Uncas time to stand up and recover. They both stood before attacking each other again, grappling for the upper hand. Magua pulled back to swing his hatchet overhead again, but mid-swing Uncas rushed him, grabbed his back, and thrust his knife into Magua's stomach. The Wendat grunted, raising his hatchet despite the pain. He went to swing it again and Uncas pushed him away.

Magua staggered away from Uncas and the rock face, his back to the cliff behind him. Hawkeye finished loading his rifle, and he trained it on Magua's chest. Magua looked between the men and Cora...dearest Cora, who stared up at him stoically with a tear-stained face. Neither man moved to shoot or attack Magua. They just watched to see what he would do next. He locked eyes with Cora, pleading with her.

"Was there ever a chance, Cora?" he asked. His eyebrows were knitted together, his lips slightly parted.

"When we met, before I first saw you kill, you were kind, and you were intelligent, and you were beautiful."

"And now?" he asked, his voice breaking.

"Your kindness and intelligence have been marred by your brutality, and any beauty I saw in you vanished when you brought me my father's scalp."

"Your father did me wrong. Vengeance was my life until I met you, Cora," he argued, still trying to justify his evil act.

"So he did, but my sister did nothing and you still tried to kill her," Cora argued back, referencing the hatchet Magua had thrown at Alice in the clearing.

"Indeed, I can admit that at least. Your fair sister did not deserve my wrath, but I would scalp the gray-haired colonel ten times over!" he shouted.

"You will die, *Le Renard*. Meet death with peace," Cora said, all emotion having left her voice.

Magua's face contorted with anger as he drew his pistol from his side. Hawkeye, who had since dropped his rifle from his sights, brought it back up in a panic. Magua aimed his pistol at Uncas and pulled the trigger with a shout. However, Uncas had since ducked behind a rock, and the bullet skidded over his head. The backfire from the pistol made Magua's feet dance until he fell backward.

Uncas ran to the edge of the cliff to watch Magua's body flail as it fell, until it hit the ground far below, becoming a pile of blood and flesh, erasing all life that had inhabited it just seconds before.

Then Uncas hastened to his father's side, and Hawkeye climbed down the rock face to join them. However, Chingachgook's eyes now stared unblinking at the sky. Uncas threw his ear to his father's chest and listened for a heartbeat. Cora's body racked with sobs, she knew it was too late.

Uncas cried out as he realized his father was dead, and grabbed Hawkeye, pulling him into an embrace. The two held each other while Cora raised her hands to the heavens, praying over *Le Gros Serpent*.

49
The Last of the Mohicans

18:00

Tamenund stood from his seat, unassisted, for the first time in years. He gazed down on the body of Chingachgook, which lay facing east, his face painted red. A group of Delaware women trudged around the body, wailing in their mourning of the dead chief.

"What has happened, my son?" Tamenund asked Uncas, who stood at Chingachgook's feet. "What has happened to your father, Uncas?" Uncas put out a hand to assist the sachem down to them. Tamenund scanned Chingachgook's body. His face was so peaceful that one could hardly tell he was dead. Magua's knife had not breached his chest, so there was no evidence of the wound.

"The Huron killed him. The evil devil that stole away my Cora," Uncas looked between the sachem and his father.

"And the Huron, did he survive?"

Uncas swallowed, forcing down the lump that had settled in his throat. His gaze wandered to the heavens. "No." Tamenund nodded, gesturing for Uncas to help him down to the ground. Uncas obliged him, helping the old sachem to his father's side. When he was settled,

Tamenund laid a gentle hand on Chingachgook's forehead and muttered a few inaudible words. Then Uncas rose to his feet, glancing at his father before beginning his prayer.

"Great Manitoo, my father comes to you now. His soul now travels to meet with his brothers," Uncas said, gazing up at the sky with his arms extended above him. "Tell him to wait for me, and that I will someday join him at the grand council of our people. Tell them all that I will join them soon and take my place as the last warrior of our proud race."

Cora and Alice looked on, a slow stream of tears sliding down their faces.

"Why does my love weep?" Uncas asked, taking a step toward Cora. "That my father has gone to the happy hunting grounds? That a chief has filled his time with honor? He was good, he was dutiful, he was brave," Uncas asserted. "Who among you can deny it?" he questioned everyone present.

"The Manitoo has need of such a warrior, and he has called my father away." A solitary tear loosed from his eye, carving a new path down a foreign landscape. "My people are gone from this Earth, and I am alone."

"No!" Hawkeye said firmly. "No, Uncas, you are not alone. Gone, your people may be, but you are not alone. I have no family but you, my brother. I will follow you all my days. Your father was a good man; he was, indeed, my own father. If a day ever comes that I forget him, let the Manitoo end my days!" Hawkeye professed.

Uncas turned to his brother and tears fell, unbridled, down his cheeks. Hawkeye wrapped his arms around his brother, and they both held each other close, as if to squeeze away the pain.

"I too will follow you, Uncas," Cora said, stepping toward the grieving brothers. Uncas looked up from Hawkeye's embrace, his eyes falling on the figure of his beloved.

"You will come?" His eyes blazed with such hope that couldn't be confused for anything but love. Cora nodded, wiping the tears from her eyes.

"Wherever you go, there let me be," she reiterated.

"Cora, my heart, you will follow? You will be mine?" Uncas took her hands in his. She nodded slowly.

"I will. I love you, Uncas."

He couldn't help but smile. While Uncas was sure of Cora's affection for him, he had never dared to hope that she would love him.

"And I, you," he replied, pulling the maiden to his heart, his hand behind her head, holding her close to his chest.

Alice gazed at her sister from her seat beside their father. Cora had been pulled into a loving embrace. Alice's hand still grasped the colonel's, unable to let go and admit to herself that he was gone. She could see Hawkeye glancing between her and the couple. A small smile graced her lips as she processed her promise to the scout.

Hawkeye appeared by her side and offered her a hand to help her up. She accepted and he led her toward Uncas and Cora, who were whispering to each other.

"My brother, it is time for us to go," Hawkeye said to the young Mohican.

"Where shall we go, Hawkeye?" Alice asked, staring starry-eyed into his eyes.

"Only Uncas can answer that."

"Uncas?" Alice asked, turning toward the man.

"North, away from this land, so that we might escape this conflict," Uncas responded. The three others nodded and they walked, hand in hand, into the forest, to live a life away from the societies that had killed their fathers.

Tamenund rose from his spot beside the body of Chingachgook, turning to address the people of his tribe as the four departed. His eyes rose to the sky and scanned the clouds that sprinkled the heavens.

"It is enough," he began, addressing the crowd. "Go, children of the Lenape, the anger of the Manitoo is not done. Why should Tamenund stay? The white men are masters of the Earth, and the time of my people has not yet come again. My day has been too long. In the morning, I saw the sons of Unamis happy and strong; and yet, before the night has come, I have lived to see the last of the Mohicans."

50
Alternative Ending

Magua dragged Cora along the rocks. The dress the Wendats had given her was tight on her legs, and it kept tripping her.

"Faster. Your Mohican is getting closer," Magua spat. He was correct. Uncas sprinted along the cliff above them, quickly approaching the traveling Wendats. His brother and father trailed behind him, unable to keep up with the Bounding Deer.

"All the better that he does!" Cora yelled, wrenching her wrist from Magua's hand.

"You are mine!" Magua shouted back, snatching her wrist. "Mine or no one's!" His eyes blazed. She looked up at him, biting the inside of her mouth again. Her eyes shot to the ground and she nodded, trailing behind him again.

Magua paused to investigate the rocks ahead. One of his men suggested in Wyandot that Magua kill Cora, who was slowing them down, so that they might escape the wrath of *La Longue Carabine*. Magua whipped around to face the man.

"Any man who hurts a hair on her head will have his guts strewn over the rocks," Magua snarled.

Two shots sounded, echoing around the mountain range. Two of Magua's men fell. The Wendat chief hurried them along, dragging Cora behind him. When they reached a wider section of the cliff, Cora tore her arm from his grasp again and stepped back.

"I will go no further!" she said, staring down her captor.

"You will come with me or you will die, woman!" Magua responded.

Uncas crouched behind a rock on the cliff above, watching Magua's every move.

Below, Cora clenched her fists as she faced the Wendat chief. "Kill me if you will, but I will go no further!"

"I...I WILL kill you!" Magua reiterated.

Cora dropped her arms, seemingly defeated.

"CHOOSE!" he shouted, appearing almost scared of her.

"I have chosen," Cora stated. "It is Uncas. It has always been Uncas."

Magua's hand shook as he raised the knife above his head. Yet Cora stared at him, unmoving.

Believing Magua to be attacking his beloved, Uncas leapt from the cliff above.

Magua fell to the ground under the weight of Uncas' body. Seizing his chance, Magua's man grabbed Cora by the wrist, pulled her toward him, and buried his knife in her stomach.

Cora cried out and crumpled to the ground. Magua jumped to his feet, ignoring Uncas, who gathered himself from the jump.

"No!" Magua yelled, his anger and distress rendering his voice broken and incoherent. He knocked the knife from the hand of Cora's murderer. The man didn't even fight when Magua thrust his knife into the man's stomach, dragging it across his torso, fulfilling his earlier promise.

Uncas, now recovered, stood, finally seeing Cora's broken body lying on the ground.

"Cora..." he breathed, faltering as he took an unconscious step toward her. Magua turned on him, his knife gleaming with his victim's blood.

"This is your fault, you dog!" Uncas shouted, stumbling toward the Wendat in blind rage.

Magua easily side-stepped Uncas' wild advances. He sliced into Uncas' side, leaving the Mohican bleeding, his hand pressed to the wound. As Uncas' head cleared, his eyes drifted back to the still form of the woman he loved.

In a flash, Magua attacked him. Uncas caught the Wendat chief's hand and the two grappled, struggling to get the upper hand over each other. Magua moved his foot behind Uncas' leg and pushed harder on him, sending him falling onto his back. Then he pounced on Uncas and straddled him. He raised his knife above his head and brought it down in an attempt to stab Uncas. However, Uncas caught his wrist, and the men strained and pushed to gain the upper hand over each other, now in a stalemate.

Then the young Mohican's eyes drifted to Cora, who lay just feet away from him. His face fell. No matter if he lived or died, she was gone. He was alone.

Cora, my beloved.

Uncas stopped fighting.

"Uncas!" Chingachgook, who had just finished descending the cliff side, called out. Uncas called out for his father, his voice pitiful and hopeless. Magua retracted his knife quickly, leaving a gaping wound in the young Mohican's chest. The Wendat chief stood and faced the angry father.

Chingachgook's eyes were crazed with a mix of pain and anger. He shifted the hatchet in his hand and held up his knife with the other, advancing on the Wendat.

"Be ready to join your son in death, Mohican," Magua said, throwing a glance at Uncas, whose breath was slowing to a halt.

"You are an evil villain *Le Renard;* my son will be avenged," Chingachgook spat as he attacked, swinging his hatchet at the Wendat chief's head. Magua ducked under the blow and shoved the older man to the ground. Despite his age, Chingachgook popped straight to his feet, not giving Magua the chance to gain any advantage over him.

Magua could hear Hawkeye reloading Killdeer. He wouldn't have much time before *La Longue Carabine* was ready to kill him. The man didn't miss. *Le Renard* lunged at the older man, his knife catching Chingachgook's side. His knife gleamed in the sun, a small amount of the sagamore's blood coating the edge.

Chingachgook looked at the man for a brief second before rushing him. Magua was ready to receive him, but *Le Gros Serpent* ducked below Magua's waiting arms and slashed across the man's thigh, leaving a deep cut that bled freely down the man's leg. Magua grimaced, but fought on.

Magua swung his hatchet over his head. Chingachgook caught his wrist and then fell backward and rolled onto his back, bringing Magua with him before raising his legs and heaving the man over his head.

Now sprawled on the rocks at the edge of the cliff, Magua pushed himself to his hands and knees and assessed his situation. Hawkeye had nearly finished loading his rifle, and when he did, it would only be a matter of time before he shot Magua.

The Wendat stood and pulled his pistol from his side, lifting it. He aimed it at Chingachgook for a second. The old man paled.

"Hawkeye!"

Magua raised the pistol, passed Chingachgook, and fired at the scout. Hawkeye ducked under the rock he was behind, and the bullet skidded over his head. The backfire from the pistol made Magua's feet dance, and, unable to maintain his balance, he toppled backward over the edge of the cliff with a bloodcurdling cry.

Chingachgook ran to the edge, watching as the man flailed in the air for several seconds before his body hit the rocks below and was reduced to nothing but flesh and bones.

Upon confirming Magua was gone, Chingachgook hastened to his son's side. He let out a loud sob as he threw his head onto the young Mohican's chest, praying that he would hear even the faintest heartbeat. He was disappointed.

Three bodies lay side by side under a blanket in the Delaware village. Miss Cora Munro and *Le Cerf Agile* lay beside each other to the right of the colonel.

Tamenund stood from his seat, unassisted, for the first time in years. He looked upon the body of Uncas. Alice sat on the ground in between her father and Cora, her hands covering her face as she sobbed. Delaware women trudged around Uncas' body, wailing in their mourning of the dead chief.

"What has happened, my son?" Tamenund asked Chingachgook, who stood at Uncas' feet. "What has happened to your son, Chingachgook?" Chingachgook put out a hand to assist the sachem down to them. Tamenund's eyes scanned Uncas' body. His face was so peaceful, that one could hardly tell he was dead.

"The Huron killed him." Chingachgook's eyes scanned between the sachem and his son.

"And the Huron, did he survive?"

Chingachgook's gaze wandered to the heavens. "No."

Tamenund nodded, gesturing for Tessouat to help him down to the ground. The man obliged him, helping the old sachem to Uncas' side. When he was settled, Tamenund laid a gentle hand on the young Mohican's forehead and muttered a few inaudible words. Then Chingachgook rose to his feet, glancing at his son before beginning his prayer.

"Great Manitoo, my son comes to you now. His soul now travels to meet with my brothers," Chingachgook said, gazing up at the sky with his arms extended above him. "Tell him to wait for me, that I am sorry I cannot be with him, and that I will someday join him at the grand council of our people. Tell them all that I will join them soon and take my place as the last warrior of our proud race."

Alice watched, a slow stream of tears sliding down her face.

"Why does my daughter weep?" Chingachgook asked, taking a step toward the lady. "That a great warrior has gone to the happy hunting grounds? That a chief has filled his time with honor? He was good, he was dutiful, he was brave," Chingachgook asserted. "Who among you can deny it?" he asked, his eyes shooting around to question all those present.

"The Manitoo has need of such a warrior, and he has called my son away." A solitary tear loosed from his eye, carving a new path down a foreign landscape. "My people are gone from this Earth, and I am alone."

"No!" Hawkeye said firmly. "No, father, you are not alone. Gone, your people may be, but you are not alone. I have no family but you. I will follow you all my days. Uncas was a good man; he was, indeed, my own brother. If a day ever comes that I forget him, let the Manitoo end my days!" Hawkeye professed. Hawkeye approached his father, tears streaming down his face. Chingachgook wrapped his arms around his surrogate son, squeezing him hard.

Alice watched the men embrace, then pushed herself to her feet. She approached the two of them, tears still falling down her cheeks. "Dear Chingachgook, you will not be alone, I swear it! As long as you will have me, I will stay with you and Hawkeye."

Chingachgook pulled away from his son and gazed down at the gentle girl. "Oh my dear Chulëntët. Of course you may join us!" The man approached her and pulled her into an embrace, running a gentle hand over her hair as she sobbed into his chest.

"My father," Hawkeye began. "It is time for us to go."

"Where shall we go?" Alice asked the woodsman.

"Only my father can answer that question."

"North, away from this land, so that we might escape this conflict," Chingachgook responded. Alice and Hawkeye nodded, and they all walked into the forest to live a life away from the societies that had killed their families.

Tamenund rose from his spot beside the body of Uncas, turning to address the people of his tribe as the three departed. His eyes rose to the sky and scanned the clouds that sprinkled the heavens.

"It is enough," he began, addressing the crowd. "Go, children of the Lenape; the anger of the Manitoo is not done. Why should Tamenund stay? The white men are masters of the Earth, and the time of my people has not yet come again. My day has been too long. In the morning, I saw the sons of Unamis happy and strong; and yet, before the night has come, have I lived to see the last of the Mohicans."

About the Author

J ohannah Jahn is a historical fiction writer. She is in University
studying Criminology and is en route to receiving a commission
as an officer in the United States Air Force.

Johannah loves traveling; her favorite trips have been to Italy and
Germany. She enjoys playing most sports, but loves soccer and tennis
above all.

Johannah is a Roman Catholic and developing her relationship
with God is one of the most important parts of her life.